All Pepped Up

Pepper Jones Book #2

By Ali Dean

Editor: Leanne Rabesa

http://editingjuggernaut.wordpress.com/

Cover: Sarah Foster

http://sprinklesontopstudios.com/

Proof Reader: Nicole Bailey

http://proofbeforeyoupublish.com

Chapter 1

My heart rate picks up as I take in the cars parked nearly half a mile from the party. This isn't just a little get-together. I can pretend like a bigger party is better because we might have a chance of going unnoticed, but that's impossible with Jace at my side. By the end of the night, everyone from Brockton and the surrounding towns will know that Jace Wilder is my boyfriend.

My success during the last cross country running season pulled me out from my comfortable obscurity, but now I'm entering a whole new level of spotlight. It's about to get real.

We park in Remy's driveway. Somehow, that parking space is miraculously available, as though everyone knew, or hoped, that Jace would show up, and made sure he had the best access to the party.

As soon as we step into the kitchen, people surround us – or Jace, to be more specific. I just happen to be standing next to him. He hasn't been out much since he began spending more time with me. But I doubt that the attention bestowed on him tonight is especially unusual.

I don't pay much attention to the conversation around us and instead simply try to absorb what it must be like to be Jace Wilder. Within minutes of his arrival, the number of people in the kitchen has tripled. We're backed up against the island counter in the center of the kitchen, and it's impossible not to feel slightly claustrophobic. I lean toward Jace, seeking comfort from the loud voices, sweaty bodies, and the smell of alcohol.

If I ever had doubts about Jace's magnetism, they've evaporated. He's like a celebrity. Everyone wants to touch him, talk to him, be able to tell their friends they've had his attention for a moment. I've never found it particularly disturbing, until now. As his girlfriend, what does this mean for me?

I could tell Remy's house was big from the outside, but as we make our way into a gigantic room filled with people, I begin to comprehend how he's able to throw such a huge party. There are people *everywhere*.

As Jace's close friend and co-captain of the varsity baseball team, Remy Laroche is one of the most popular guys at Brockton Public High School. I've been to a party at his house –

rather, in his backyard – once before with Ryan Harding, my ex-boyfriend. But it didn't prepare me for the mass of people tonight. Judging by the number of faces I've never seen before, it's not just Brockton Public kids here.

Jace must sense my anxiety because he pulls me closer to him. I inhale his comforting smell and glance up. He touches my chin with his index finger and raises my face to see me better.

"Hey. Do you wanna play pool?" Jace asks.

"I've never played."

"Come on. I'll teach you."

When we get to the table, Ben's arranging the balls into a diamond. Ben Hughes, along with Connor Locke, Ryan Harding and Remy Laroche, make up the elite group of senior guys at Brockton Public. Oh, and Jace Wilder – that goes without saying.

Ben greets me with a warm smile. "It's great to see you, Pepper."

"Thanks." I smile back uncertainly. Last time I showed up at Remy's house for a party, they had not made me feel welcome. That was back in September. And I was on a sort-of-first-date with Ryan.

"I was hoping you guys would show up. Glad you could make it, man." Ben does the fist-bump thing with Jace before handing him a pool cue.

Are they really just accepting me into their group like it's no big deal? Jace must have told his friends about us already, because they don't seem surprised to see me.

It was my idea to hold off making our relationship public knowledge. At first it was to protect Ryan's feelings. Ryan was my first boyfriend – but not the first boy I fell for.

I broke up with Ryan in December, after we both won the individual titles at the National Cross Country meet. The next day, Jace decided not to wait any longer. It was a long time coming. I'd crushed on Jace for years, and it was a sweet revelation when I discovered that my feelings were reciprocated.

I never thought I'd be that girl who jumped from one boy to the next, but I guess I am now.

My decision to keep my relationship with Jace a secret for nearly two months wasn't all about Ryan, though. It will be a lot harder with our relationship out in the open. People accept my friendship with Jace, even though we don't run in the same crowds, but what will happen now that we're dating?

Jace shows me how to hold the pool cue, and we walk through a game together, just the two of us, before teaming up against Remy and Ben. I *really* like playing pool with Jace. It gives him an excuse to touch me. Not that he needs one.

He leans behind me whenever it's my turn, helping me aim, or at least that's what he says. Every time his hips touch mine and I feel his breath in my ear, I get a little dizzy.

"Mr. Wilder," I whisper when I feel his chest against my back, "while I appreciate your assistance, I think it's doing more to throw me off than help." I continue looking ahead as I feel his lips brush along my neck.

"Is that so?" He pushes his hips closer to me as I adjust my hold. "Try to sink the purple one in the far left."

I miss. Fortunately, Jace is an excellent pool player and he makes up for my misses when it's his turn. Watching him shoot is quite the turn-on, and by the time the game ends, I'm a hot mess.

As soon as I finish my beer, a guy I don't recognize replaces it with another one. I glance at Jace, who nods at the guy in thanks.

"Um, I don't know that guy. Should I really drink a beer from him?" I asked Jace quietly, so no one else can hear my dorky paranoia.

Jace grins. "I love that you're careful, and you're right, you shouldn't take drinks from guys you don't know. Or any guy, for that matter. But it's okay if I'm with you. He knows you're with me. No one's gonna mess with you." He nuzzles my neck and I tentatively sip the beer in a futile attempt to cool my libido. I believe Jace. I trust him.

"Let's play ping pong next," I suggest.

"Oh, really? You think you might be able to take me?"

"I'm much better at ping pong. Charlie has a table at his place so I've got some skills. Plus, you won't be able to distract me so bad." Charlie Owens is one of my teammates and he's dating my best friend, Zoe Burton, so we spend a lot of time together.

"Is that what you think? We'll see about that." He flashes a knowing smirk and I raise my eyebrows in challenge.

"Show me what you got, Wilder. But first, I need the ladies' room."

"It's down the hall, want me to go with?" Jace waggles his eyebrows.

"Nooo … " I roll my eyes.

"Okay, but you can always change your mind after the ping pong game. Here, let me hold your beer for you."

I make my way down the hall and discover a line for the bathroom. My nerves return when I lean against the wall and take in my surroundings. I was distracted by the exhilaration I always feel when I'm with Jace. But without his nearby presence, I'm edgy around all these people I hardly know.

I wish I had my phone on me to provide a distraction. I'm staring at the ground when wet naked feet with red painted toenails stop in my line of vision.

Madeline Brescoll stands before me in a white string bikini, drops of water dripping down her cleavage. How is she so perfectly tan in the middle of winter? And why is she always wearing a damn bathing suit?

Madeline is a bombshell, plain and simple. The kind of gorgeous that turns heads. Jace's female equivalent in some ways. I hate that I just thought that.

Madeline is also incredibly wealthy; her dad owns one of the largest breweries in the United States. But she's also known to be quite vicious. I don't know details, but I do know she's been the queen bee – "B for bitch" as my friend Zoe likes to say – at Lincoln Academy for most of her high school career. That's not an easy feat, as most of the kids at the private high school come from money and high-powered families. Now that Madeline's a senior, nobody gets in her way.

She's been tolerant of me, if not overly nice, when we've crossed paths before. But judging by the look in her eyes now, she's not pleased to see me.

When the door to the bathroom opens she cuts everyone in line and walks in with her sidekicks - Serena and Emma - behind her. No one complains.

After several minutes, they reemerge. I hope they'll ignore me but I'm not so fortunate.

"So, Jace gave you permission to come out again, huh?" Madeline doesn't waste time with fake niceties.

I shrug, unwilling to egg her on. She's speaking loud enough for people around us to listen. Has word already spread that Jace is more than just my friend? When it comes to news about Jace Wilder, I wouldn't be surprised if everyone at the party knew he had a girlfriend within five minutes of our arrival.

"He likes to dote on you. I don't know what he sees, but it's about time he gave in to your infatuation and let you have what you want." Madeline's words confirm that news travels fast. She pauses, glancing around to ensure she has an audience. "He'll get off on whatever little game he has going with you, and when he's had his fun, he'll be back in my bed."

I gape at her. Speechless.

Serena takes a step forward. "You know he always goes back to Maddie. He can't get enough of her."

Emma chimes in with, "Jace likes to love and leave but not with Maddie. He always wants another piece." Emma's voice is overtly nonchalant, like she's just stating the way of the universe.

Madeline shrugs. "I know the score. He needs to spice things up a little with you, but he'll get bored. He always does."

"Except with you," Serena says to Madeline with a giggle, and Emma joins in her knowing laughter.

Madeline takes a step forward and tilts her cup toward my chest, letting red liquid pour onto me before I can move out of the way. I'm pressed against the wall with nowhere to turn as I watch the stain spread over my new green dress.

"Oops," she says. "Someone must have bumped me."

"Too bad it's cranberry and vodka. Not sure that will come out," Emma says as the girls walk away.

"Here, you can go next," the girl in front of me in line says sympathetically.

I quickly lock myself in the bathroom. Swallowing the lump in my throat, I look at myself in the mirror. The green dress I bought just for this occasion is ruined. Blinking back tears, I scrub uselessly at the red stains with a wet towel.

Leaning against the bathroom counter, I close my eyes and try to pull myself together. I know I shouldn't let petty mean girls get to me, but their reaction is exactly what I've been fearing for the last two months since Jace and I became a couple.

There's no denying how ridiculous those girls are, but it doesn't make their attack on me any less real. Because that's exactly what it was – an attack. A public declaration that things are only temporary between me and Jace, and I don't really belong in his social realm. And no matter how absurd she is, people pay attention to Madeline.

Chapter 2

After doing the business I originally came to the bathroom for, I splash my face with cold water. My cheeks are blotchy but I can't spend any more time in the bathroom with such a long line. And Jace is bound to come looking for me.

I open the bathroom door tentatively, afraid Madeline will be waiting to torment me some more. She's not in sight, so I walk down the hallway toward Jace with my arms crossed over my chest in a futile attempt to hide the gigantic stain on my dress.

I really want to go home. I can't spend the rest of the night in this dress, and Madeline's words, as much as I wish I could ignore them, hurt me. I have enough insecurity about why Jace is with me without her opinion. Is this some sort of game for him? Just a way to change things up? Try a new MO before starting college?

But when his eyes lock with mine from across the room and I watch them light up in happiness, then soften with concern at my expression, I know it's more than that. I mean something to him.

Madeline is standing by him in her stupidly sexy white bathing suit, brushing her boobs against his chest. She looks silly with everyone around her fully dressed. A hot tub's visible through the screen doors, but her unwillingness to put on even a towel makes her appear desperate. Like her body is all she has to offer. And Jace isn't even paying attention to her assets. He walks right past her toward me.

"Pep, what happened?" He strokes my cheek.

I shrug. "Someone bumped into me and spilled their drink. It's no big deal."

"Who was it?"

"I don't know. No one I knew." He's protected me from so much already – frequently to the point of overkill – at times, I've wished he'd back off. I want to handle Madeline and her friends on my own.

"We can go home if you want, but I'm sure Remy's older sister has clothes you can borrow. She's away at college."

I don't want to go home anymore. I want to show Madeline that she didn't ruin my night. Besides, Jace hasn't been out with his friends in a while, and we were having a great time.

"Remy!" Jace calls over to the pool table where Remy is flirting with Serena – or is it Emma? I get them mixed up.

Remy ditches her and walks over to us. "What's up?"

"You got any clothes Pepper can borrow? Maybe something of Amelia's?"

"Yeah, no problem. Come on up."

Remy leads us up a couple of flights of stairs, explaining that his sister has more clothes than she could fit in her dorm room at college. We walk into her room and my jaw drops when I see the walk-in closet.

"She's a little bigger than you, but I'm sure you can find something that works. Go at it." He gestures to the walk-in before heading back to the party.

Jace watches me as I sort through the hangers. "Here, take off your dress and I'll rinse it to try to get the stain out." His voice is tense, and I follow his order without protest.

When I stand before him in nothing but leggings, cowboy boots, and my favorite lacy push-up bra that actually makes it look like I have cleavage, I expect some sort of reaction. He's seen me in a bathing suit, but never in my underwear. Jace just clenches his jaw, takes the dress from my hand, and stomps off to the bathroom.

Maybe it's because I'm already upset, but I have to swallow down another set of tears that burn to spill out. His rejection hurts. Especially after what Madeline said. *He needs to spice things up a little with you, but he'll get bored. He always does.*

Maybe he's already bored. We kiss a lot, and there's plenty of touching, but our clothes always stay on. Maybe I'm just not experienced enough, not sexy enough, and that's why he never takes it further.

He'll get off on whatever little game he has going with you and when he's had his fun, he'll be back in my bed.

I yank a white tee shirt off a hanger and pull it over my head. It's loose-fitting and hangs off one shoulder, exposing my lacy bra strap. It reaches mid-thigh, and looks sexy with my leggings and cowboy boots. Well, maybe not Madeline Brescoll-sexy, but you can see the outline of my purple bra through the thin material, and that's pretty scandalous for me.

I spin around when I catch Jace checking me out in the mirror. I might not have much more time with him, and I want to make it count. Keep him un-bored for as long as possible.

"Thanks for rinsing my dress," I whisper when I approach him. He watches me apprehensively as I run my fingers down his chest, feeling the firm planes and then the muscular ridges of his abs before letting my hands settle on his belt buckle.

He sucks in a breath. "Pepper, are you going to tell me why you were so upset? It's not like you to get all bent out of shape from someone accidentally spilling on you. What happened?"

Jace knows me well enough to recognize the signs that I was crying. "I don't want to talk about it," I murmur. Standing on my tiptoes, I reach up to kiss his ear and along his neck.

"Pepper." My name sounds like a moan. Jace grasps my hips, lifts me up and places me a foot away from him. He puts his hands on his hips. "Stop distracting me. I want to know what happened. I'll make it better."

"You already did. See?" I gesture to my outfit. "Don't I look nice?"

"You're gorgeous, Pepper. Always. And just so you know, don't think you can wear anything like that unless I'm around."

I suppress a grin. At times like this, his protective streak is sweet.

Jace's jaw ticks, his giveaway that his temper is brewing. "Well?" he asks.

"Well what?"

"What happened to make you upset?"

I sigh. "Jace, I'm over it, okay? Sometimes I need to fight my own battles. This is girl stuff."

"Girl stuff?" Jace asks doubtfully. "What, you think I can only handle guys?"

I place a hand on his chest. "You've been with a lot of girls, okay? And, since you're so amazing and all, the girls who didn't get to keep you are going to be a little bitchy, that's all. It's nothing I can't handle." I sound more confident than I feel. If only this was as simple as a scorned girl. Perhaps it is. But it's hard to shrug off a girl – no, a woman – like Madeline Brescoll.

Jace steps closer and lifts me up so that my legs wrap around his waist. "I won't get involved if you don't want me to." He kisses the tip of my nose. "For now," he adds.

I tilt my head to the side and raise my eyebrows.

Jace starts walking out of the closet and toward the queen bed. "Girls can be brutal. I've witnessed it. If I hear about more bitchiness toward you, I'm not gonna let it happen." He leans down, placing me on my back, and hovers over me. "But you can't let them get to you, Pep." His green eyes search mine. "It's only ever been you. No matter what other girls say, you're all that matters. It's always been like that. I'm gonna keep trying to show you."

"All right," I whisper. But Emma's voice echoes in my head. *Jace likes to love and leave but not with Maddie. He always wants another piece.*

When his lips meet mine, I decide I'll simply make him want me too. I arch my back and press myself to him, grasping his shoulders tightly and urging him against me. If he's surprised by my aggressive response, he doesn't show it. He responds by catching my lower lip with his teeth.

I glide my hands down his sculpted back and slip my hands beneath the band of his boxer briefs. I've never done this before and it feels amazing to be this close.

I hear Jace's ragged breathing in my ear as I kiss and nip at his neck, and it emboldens me to continue. If it feels this good to touch his bare skin here…

I slide my hands up and around to the front of his pants and quickly open the button and pull down the zipper. I'm nervous, and I know if I think about it too much I'll chicken out. My hands slip underneath his boxers and Jace freezes. I can't even hear him breathing. I take him in my hands.

"Oh!" I gasp as I let my hands glide up and down. It's... bigger than I expected. "Jace?" I ask shakily.

"Yeah?" He sounds like he's in pain.

"Um... does it... you know... fit?" I bite out. I scrunch my eyes in embarrassment. But seriously, it's hard to fathom how it could possibly work.

I feel Jace's chest vibrate with laughter. "Yeah."

I run my hands over the soft skin. "Ah, fuck," Jace grunts and jerks his hips a little. "Pepper." He says my name like he's in agony before rolling to his side, slipping out of my grasp and putting distance between us.

He breathes heavily for a moment. "I can't think when you're touching me like that," he says finally. He sounds like he just sprinted the length of a football field.

"Is that a good thing?" Although I already know the answer.

"Well, it feels amazing, but I don't like losing control with you, Pep," he says quietly. "You were just upset, and then" – he runs his hands through his jet black hair and down his face – "ahhh... I want to be good for you Pepper. I don't want you moving faster than you're comfortable with because of what some bitchy girls said."

I swallow. He knows me too well. "You're right, Jace. I wanted to prove to myself that you wanted me. I wanted to make you want me. I mean, I liked it. Touching you was..." I laugh and look at the ceiling. "Well, I want to do it again. But maybe we should stop tonight. We're here to hang out."

He holds my head in his hands and turns me so I'm facing him. "Don't ever doubt that I want you. I do. So much. But I want to do it right. I want this to last. I can be patient with you because I want all of it, all of you, over and over again. There's no need to rush."

"I know I'm being silly. I don't like being a girl who needs her boyfriend's constant reassurance. I'll try not to be so high maintenance."

"Believe me, you are not high maintenance. I wish I didn't have the kind of past that makes you doubt me, or us, or yourself. But I'm gonna try to protect you from it as much as I can." We gaze at each other for a moment longer. "I just need a sec before we go down there, to uh, calm down." Jace glances down at his open pants. "That should be all the proof you need," he says with a smirk.

"I don't know. You were able to stop, after all. Maybe I should follow through to make sure there's no mistake about who you want," I say, trying out a mock-seductive voice. I'm kidding, of course. Sort of. Jace's hooded eyes seem to be taking me seriously. The fire that started burning is still aflame, and I need a bucket of cold water dumped on me if I'm going to move from this bed any time tonight.

Jace grabs my hands and brings them over my head as he rolls back on me. He leaves my hands locked above my head as he devours me with a scorching kiss. But he quickly breaks the kiss and hops up from the bed with a growl. "Woman!" He backs away from the bed as he tucks himself in and buttons his pants. The bulge is still evident and I grin. "What you do to me!" He groans as if I was torturing him. And perhaps I was. My confidence, in that area of our relationship at least, is restored.

I jump out of bed. "Ping pong?" I ask.

A doubles match is going on when we get back downstairs, and I finish another beer while we wait our turn. It looks like others are waiting to play winner, but they give us the paddles. Jeez, I could get used to this kind of treatment. I'm feeling a little buzzed from the two beers, and probably from the earlier make-out session, but I'm actually pretty good at ping pong and I want to give Jace a decent game.

"I got winner." I hear Wesley Jamison's voice as he heads our way.

Wes's arrival turns a few heads, mostly female, and I'm happy to have some of the attention taken away from Jace. Wesley is tall with a powerful lean body and striking good looks, like Jace, but not quite as devastating. His blonde hair and easy smile sets girls at ease, another difference from Jace, whose dark features and piercing green eyes put most girls on edge. In a good way.

The three of us have hung out a few times over the last couple of months. He was one of the first to learn about Jace and I. It's surprisingly easy to fall into the comfortable friendship we'd had before high school started. Before Wes and Jace had some sort of falling out that I never heard the explanation for.

Wes lifts me up in a hug when he reaches me. "What's up, Pep?"

"Hey, Wes. You weren't up to no good, were you?"

He laughs. "I'm always up to no good." But he knows what I mean.

Wes and Jace were dealing drugs until a couple of months ago, but as far as I know, they managed to cut themselves off from that world entirely.

"All right, Wes, get your hands off my girl," Jace calls from the other side of the table.

Wes shakes his head at Jace's comment but complies.

Jace and I play point for point and it appears he's actually trying, though I wouldn't put it past him to be faking it to humor me.

"Damn, your girlfriend's got skills," Ben says from the sideline.

I know it's not my skills or the close match that draws the crowd, though. Halfway through, Jace tossed his shirt to the side. He smirked at me and I knew he was trying to mess with my concentration. I'm on my third beer, and I'm actually starting to break a sweat. So with alcohol-induced boldness I roll up the oversized tee shirt above my belly button and tie it off to the side. I can play this game too.

It's not my bare stomach that distracts Jace, but his annoyance that others are seeing it. But hey, when your boyfriend has six-pack abs, perfect pecs, and the biceps of a quarterback, you have to fight back with what you can. And I know jealousy is a weakness of his. It doesn't come from any insecurity – definitely not that – but from something far more painful he's buried deep. I might be the only one who sees it, though I expect my Gran understands Jace's demons too. And perhaps Wes.

By the time we get to match point, it seems like the entire party is focused on us. People cheer and girls whistle and yell inappropriate remarks at Jace. Match point goes back and forth several times until I finish it off with an ace to the far back corner.

Jace stalks around the table toward me and I stand my ground, grinning like an idiot. He grabs me around the waist on my bare skin, and I love the feel of his big hands on me.

"You are really sexy when you get all competitive on me," he growls low in my ear.

"What can I say? I've got a competitive spirit," I reply playfully.

"Oh? We'll have a rematch. But without the audience," he murmurs.

"Promise?"

Wes thumps Jace on the shoulder, snapping us out of our flirtations. "All right, lovebirds, looks like I'm taking on little hot shot here."

"We'll see about that," I retort, stepping away from Jace. Once out of our safe cocoon and the distraction of the competitive ping pong match, I feel the weight of the eyes from our audience.

Jace seems to notice as well because he tugs my shirt out of its knot so it hangs below my butt again.

"You know, you can put your shirt back on now," I remind him.

Jace smirks. "Maybe I like knowing I have your attention."

Before Wes can serve, Madeline saunters up to him. "Hey! I know! We can play doubles." She claps her hands excitedly. The beach wrap she's got on over her bikini doesn't do much to hide her bouncing boobs. The boys in the audience don't seem to mind.

Wes shrugs and looks at Jace for approval. Jace nods slowly but he narrows his eyes suspiciously at Madeline.

It isn't much of a game at first, because Madeline can't seem to hit the ball over the net and onto the table. Each time it flies in the wrong direction she giggles and touches Wesley to apologize. It's hard to believe anyone is that bad at ping pong, especially the Lincoln Academy varsity tennis team captain.

Eventually, Wes gets annoyed and starts hitting the balls that land on her side. But then Madeline gushes at his athletic prowess and rubs herself all over him. She's putting on a show. But for whom?

I would think that the boys in the audience would lose interest in Madeline once they see she has her sights set on Wesley for the night. But no, apparently they love watching her air-brained flirtations and the way she manages to shake her booty and boobs with every movement. Even I'm a little impressed. The girl knows how to rock her body.

And once Wes realizes the game is hopeless, and that Madeline is seriously coming on to him, he starts to reciprocate the attention. I glance at Jace. His jaw is clenched and he doesn't look amused.

Is he jealous?

I tilt my head, trying to evaluate Jace's expression. He glances at me. "You ready to head out, Pep?" he asks. Though he's asked my opinion, I can tell he's over it. I am too.

I swallow, and realize there's a lump in my throat. Madeline's getting to me, but I can't let her see it. "Yeah, okay," I agree.

Jace takes my hand and leads me upstairs, not bothering with goodbyes. He doesn't say anything until we're in the car and pulling out of the driveway.

"It was Madeline, wasn't it?" he asks.

I glance at him. The sharp lines of his jaw and forehead are silhouetted by the streetlights.

"She was the one messing with you earlier tonight," he clarifies.

Sighing, I turn my gaze back to the road. "It doesn't matter, Jace."

"Of course it matters, Pep. She has no right to play games with you." He stops the car at a stop sign and looks over at me. "And it's only happening because of me. That's not right."

"I hardly ever run into her. I'll handle it," I assure him.

I hope his lack of response means he's dropped it, but I know him better than that. Jace doesn't like to leave things out of his control. Especially when it involves me.

Chapter 3

Pancakes at the Wilders' house on Sunday mornings have become routine over the past two months. Now that Jace's whereabouts aren't so unpredictable – not to mention morally questionable – Dave and I can count on a hearty breakfast around 10:00 in the morning with Jace and his dad, Jim. Sometimes Wes swings by, too.

The Wilders have been our neighbors on Shadow Lane my whole life. They live just down the street from our apartment building.

After trudging the short way to their house in my pajamas and snow boots, I brush off Dave's paws and open the front door. It smells like coffee and blueberry pancakes.

"Aw, lucky you, Dave," I coo. "You won't get left out this week like you did with the chocolate ones last week." Dave's ears perk up. "That's right, no chocolate for doggies." I shake my finger before pulling off my snow boots. A female pair of boots sits by the door, and I figure Jim's girlfriend Sheila must be over.

Dave follows me into the kitchen. My jacket is halfway off when my gaze lands on the woman sitting at the small breakfast table. Those are *Jace's* green eyes. Unlike Jace and Jim, the woman is petite, even bony. She's wearing a long sweater and a colorful hippie-style skirt. Her thick black hair flows down to her waist. Though her cheeks are a bit sunken and she has dark circles under her eyes, the woman looks young – at least, young for the mother of an eighteen-year-old.

"Good morning, Pepper," Jim greets me. He's flipping pancakes, like it's any other morning.

"Hey, Jim." I head toward him for a quick hug, unwilling to deviate from our routine for *her*.

The anger vibrating inside me is startling. I had no idea I felt so strongly about this woman – a woman I don't even remember. But she abandoned Jace when he was only four years old, and there can't possibly be a good enough reason to justify that.

So, I ignore her. "Where's Jace?" I ask.

"He'll be up in a minute," Jim tells me. He sips his coffee before breaking the ice. "Pepper, you probably don't remember Jace's mother, Annie, do you?"

I shake my head.

"I remember you, Pepper. And your Gran, Bunny. How is she?" Annie asks from her spot – *my* spot – at the table.

"She's good." My voice is monotone. How *dare* she come in here acting like she never left? Does she even know how much her abandonment has affected Jace? I've never spoken to Jace about his mother, but there's a reason he craves power and control, especially in his interactions with other people. He won't let himself be abandoned again. He'll control who gets hurt. And it won't be him.

It's something I've always known about Jace, but never thought about much. It's just the way he is. And it hurts him to be like that. Whether he'll admit it or not.

Jace shuffles up the stairs in his sweatpants and a University of Colorado tee shirt. The Wilders live in a bi-level; Jace has the downstairs to himself.

His face is carefully expressionless, but he cracks a smile when he sees me. I walk toward him and nestle into his chest. Does he share my anger toward his mother? I realize how utterly clueless I am about Jace's feelings toward her. Until now, we've acted like she doesn't exist.

Dave shoves his head between our knees, trying to sandwich himself between us. "Hey buddy, you want in on the hug?" Jace asks him. We let Dave wiggle between us for a moment.

When Jace heads over to the table, I follow his lead and sit down at the fourth chair – not my usual spot, thanks to *Annie.*

Apparently Jace already faced his mother this morning, because he proceeds to pour maple syrup over his pancakes without any sort of outburst. I'm craving an outburst. I want him to throw something, scream, yell, let it all out. But no, the Wilders are acting like this is no big deal.

"So, how long are you in Brockton for?" Jace asks.

"Oh, I'm moving back," Annie announces. "Living at a friend's place for now, and looking for a job."

Jace shovels some pancakes onto my plate, trying to shake me from staring dumbly at him.

"What kind of job?" Jim asks as he takes a seat with another plate full of pancakes. He slides a glass of orange juice over to me.

"Oh, I'm flexible. I have some experience waitressing, but I'll just have to see who's hiring." Annie brushes her long hair over her shoulder and takes a small bite from her plate.

"Pep works at the Tavern in the summers. Do you think they might be hiring?" Jim asks me.

I shrug. "Maybe."

Why isn't anyone else angry with this woman? My appetite has vanished. I tear off a piece of pancake and toss it to Dave, who's waiting patiently under the table.

"What are you two up to today?" Annie asks brightly.

I flick my eyes to Jace.

"Probably work out, do some homework," Jace answers casually. He must be trying to impress her, because he hardly ever does homework. Sometimes he'll watch football at my house while I'm studying, but football season is over now. Why is he treating her like she's his mother? She doesn't deserve it.

"It's just so great that you two are still friends. You spent a lot of time together as toddlers, you know?"

She went there. To the time when she was around. When my parents were still alive. That time period is not discussed in this house.

Fortunately, Jim starts asking Annie about West Virginia, where she apparently lived for the past few years. Jace places his hand on my thigh and squeezes. It's absurd that I'm the one who needs reassurance in this situation.

We finish our breakfast, catching up on life as though Annie is just an old friend, not the mother who abandoned her child. Jace and Jim walk Annie out the door when her friend comes to pick her up while I hang back to stew in frustration.

I load the dirty dishes into the dishwasher, and Dave helps me out with a prewash by licking off the crumbs. A shiver runs up my spine when Jace tugs me back toward his hips.

"Jim's got plans with Sheila, so we've got the house to ourselves," he whispers in my ear.

Wiping my hands on a towel, I spin around. "Are we really going to pretend like that was normal?"

Jace ignores my question and dips his head to kiss my collarbone. "I was so distracted by these pajamas, I wasn't too concerned with anything else," Jace mumbles as his lips move up to my neck and brush along my jaw.

"Jace, an ice-cream-cone-patterned flannel pajama set is just about the farthest thing from seductive – oh!" Jace lifts me up and begins carrying me down the stairs reverse-piggyback style. He somehow manages not to trip while continuing to nibble on my neck.

My intentions to probe about Annie fly out the window when he places me on his bed and hovers over me. He let me be in control last night, at least for a moment, probably sensing that I wanted to prove something to him, or to myself, I don't know. But now, there's no question that Jace is in charge. And with the way he kisses, I'm not complaining.

***

After kissing me thoroughly and working both of us into a frenzy, Jace pulls me onto his chest for a cuddle. He always does this just when I think he might take things further.

Nestling my head into his chest, I listen to his heart beat as his chest rises and falls, wondering if he's going to say anything about Annie. I desperately want to spill my opinion, but Jace knows me well enough that I'm sure my feelings on the matter came through without me articulating them.

Jace's phone beeps and he reaches to his bedside table to check the message. "That's Wes. We're meeting at the gym in twenty."

Jace's hand draws circles on my back, and I'm in no mood to get up. "But I'm comfy," I mumble.

I feel his chest rumble with a chuckle. "You should come lift with us."

"I'm lifting with the girls tomorrow. And Dave will be sad if he misses his Sunday run with me." I just started a three-days-a-week weight lifting routine. "Besides, it's distracting having all those girls gawk at you and Wes. I swear they don't even go to the gym to work out."

Jace scoffs. "Use the negative energy toward the workout. That's what I do when I catch meatheads checking you out."

I giggle. "Yeah, but first you give them a death glare."

Jace squeezes me tighter to him. "Sometimes they need to know that looking is all they'll be doing."

UC lets Brockton Public varsity athletes use their gym on certain days of the week. When I started going to lift weights a month ago, it quickly became clear that the place is just an ogling-fest for most people.

We drag ourselves out of bed and I plop a quick kiss on his lips before scurrying out the door. Last time I lingered, Jace stripped down to change into his workout clothes right in front of me. Don't get me wrong, seeing Jace stripped down is a fine sight indeed, but the rush of lust that accompanies the view is a bit overwhelming – particularly when I'm not sure the rest of me is ready to follow my body's desires.

The wind's picked up by the time I head out for a run, but I know I'll warm up quickly. My favorite dirt trails are too snowy today so I take the bike path, which gets snow-plowed each morning.

Coach had me take three weeks off from running after Nationals in December. Since then, I've started both the weight-lifting program and building a base for track season. It's an easy five miles or so on most days, with a ten-miler once a week. The low-key schedule is enjoyable for now, but I'm sure I'll get restless soon. Track workouts don't start for another few weeks.

When we cross the bridge that takes us away from the residential streets and along the river, I let Dave off his leash. There's hardly anyone out here this time of year, and Dave likes to explore.

As expected, I heat up after several minutes. I'm wrapping my windbreaker around my waist when Dave takes off in a sprint toward an approaching couple.

"Dave!" I call out. It's not like him to do that. Hopefully these people won't get mad at me.

Fortunately, the guy crouches down to greet Dave, who eagerly licks his face like they're best friends. I jog over to apologize and see that the girl is Lisa Delany, a senior at Brockton Public.

"Oh, hi Lisa. Sorry about Dave, here. He doesn't usually approach strangers."

The guy looks up and smiles. "I'm not a stranger." Ryan.

"Oh! Sorry, I didn't recognize you!" It's probably because his gait was different from jogging slower than his usual pace with Lisa. Plus he's wearing a hat.

An awkwardness settles around us. Lisa was going after Ryan all fall, and probably while he was with me. Ryan told me he wasn't especially interested in her. But now they're running together. I feel like an intruder.

"So, I didn't know you were a runner, Lisa," I say in what I hope is a pleasant voice, trying to ease the tension.

"I'm just getting into it. Ryan's helping me. I figured it'd be good cross-training for tennis." That's right. Lisa is captain of the Brockton Public tennis team.

Her long blonde hair is pulled into a ponytail and she has a hot pink ear warmer around her head. "Nice. I'll let you guys get going before we start to freeze up."

Ryan stands up from petting Dave and waves before jogging off with Lisa. I head off in the other direction, Dave leading the way, and realize I hardly spoke to Ryan. Does he know about Jace and me? Is he with Lisa now?

I don't like the idea of Ryan and Lisa together. But it can't be jealousy. I broke up with *him*. But I still care about him, and he's too good for Lisa. That must be it.

Chapter 4

I recognize the Burton family's minivan parked on the street when I finish up the loop, and I know Zoe must have stopped by. Jogging up the stairs, I kick off my snowy sneakers in the hallway and head inside.

"Yo!" Zoe calls from the couch. She's made herself comfortable with a mug of tea, her feet propped up on the coffee table.

"What's up?" I plop down next to her. "What are you watching?"

"HGTV. You know anyone can come in here and just take whatever they want, right?" Zoe asks.

I shrug. "I was only out for a little bit. We hardly ever lock up and nothing's happened yet."

"Go take a shower, you stink," she tells me.

"Yes ma'am," I reply with a salute. Fifteen minutes later I find Zoe painting her toenails in my bedroom.

"I saw Ryan on the bike path," I tell her as I unwrap the towel from my head and rub my wet hair. "Guess who he was with?"

Zoe looks up. "Lisa Delany?"

I pause with my hairbrush in hand. "How'd you know?"

Zoe shrugs. "Something's been going on with them for a couple of weeks. You've just been too wrapped up in Jace to notice." She blows on her toes before adding, "Not that you ever pay attention to who's with whom anyway. But Ryan's different."

"Jeez, now I feel dumb for insisting on keeping me and Jace a secret for so long." I tug the brush through my hair. Although, after last night, it's probably best that I avoided the wrath of Madeline Brescoll. No need to get into that with Zoe. She'll just get all worked up.

"Nah, it was better you waited. You're the one who broke the poor kid's heart," Zoe says nonchalantly, but I catch the evil little smirk on her lips in the mirror.

"Yeah, yeah. Enough of that already. You know it's different with Jace. It was the right move, admit it."

She flexes her toes in front of her. "Do you think it's too bright?"

"Zoe, it's February. No one's going to see your bare feet."

"Except for Charles." She wiggles her eyebrows knowingly.

I throw the hairbrush at her. "Gross." We were buddies with our teammate Charlie Owens for years before he and Zoe started dating this past fall. They're cute together, but that doesn't mean I want details.

"But you know I'm cool with you and Jace. It's just weird because he's still, like, *the* Jace Wilder to me. Maybe now that you guys are out in the open we can all hang out more together and I'll be able to think of him as a real person."

I slide on my fluffy red slippers and check my cell to see if Jace has called. No messages. A light snow has started falling outside, and Zoe and I decide to forgo homework in favor of baking cookies. It's just that kind of a day.

Gran comes home later in the afternoon with groceries and a baking agenda of her own.

"Where's the Christmas music?" is the first thing out of her mouth. When it snows, Gran puts on Hanson Brothers' Christmas Carols, no matter the time of year. Yes, *those* Hanson Brothers.

By dinnertime, we've baked multiple batches of cookies and none of us are hungry for a real meal. My belly is full of batter.

Gran insists we invite some friends over to help with the cookies – eating them, that is. Zoe sends a text to Charlie, who is "studying" with Rollie and Omar. Apparently Zoe and I aren't the only ones in procrastination mode, because they seem happy enough to drop the studying; they show up at our apartment twenty minutes later.

Roland Fowler and Omar Hernandez are both juniors on the cross team, and we've been friends since freshman year. Omar plays baseball in the spring instead of running track like the rest of us, but he still spends most of his time hanging out with the running crowd.

Jace doesn't answer when I call, which surprises me. We usually meet up on Sunday evenings. I send him a text message about the cookies, knowing he won't want to miss out.

"Hey," Zoe bumps her hip against mine as I open the fridge and pull out the milk. "Why so glum, chum?"

"I'm not!" I say cheerily. It's true – kind of. I'm not so much glum as I am – perplexed? Yeah, that's it. Where *is* Jace? He saw his mother for the first time in 14 years and he gave me nothing. He's got to be feeling *something.* And aren't I supposed to be his rock? At least, that's what Wesley told me when Jace went off the deep end a few months ago. I know the boy has never been an open book when it comes to his emotions, but I thought he'd at least want to hang with me, *be* with me, right now.

"Sure, chica." Zoe pats my butt, knowing well enough that I won't be getting into it with her. Jace is a private person, and it doesn't feel right talking about his mother to anyone else. At least not now, when I don't even know what the heck is going on.

The snow falling outside has picked up, and the Weather Channel is calling for a major blizzard through the night and into tomorrow. We keep the news on in the background while hanging out in the kitchen, hoping to hear about school cancellations. Since I haven't done my homework, and it doesn't look like I will, a snow day would be awesome.

It's not until 9:00 that Jace finally calls.

"Where have you been all day?" I cringe at my own question, hoping I don't sound clingy.

"Hanging out with Wes. Came over to his place after working out and just got lazy. Did you hear school's cancelled tomorrow?"

"Huh? How'd we miss that? We've been listening for it!" I call out to Zoe to check the website. "Jace says we're closed tomorrow!"

"Who all is over?" Jace asks, having heard the background noise.

"Zoe and some friends. Didn't you get my text about the cookies? I figured that would get your lazy butt over here. We made six different kinds."

"Ginger molasses?"

"You'll never know. You snooze, you lose, pal."

"Don't pal me. Is Ryan there?" Jace asks, seemingly out of the blue.

"Noooo," I respond, letting the question in my voice linger. Jace doesn't bite.

"You guys should come over to Wes's place. They canceled Lincoln too so he's having a get-together." How is he so laid back right now? My stomach would be in knots if I were him. Not to mention my mental state.

"I don't know if Gran will be down with that. The roads are really bad." The last thing I want to deal with right now is another Madeline run-in, but I'm anxious to see Jace, and that overrides anything else.

"They aren't bad yet, and you can just spend the night so you don't have to drive."

"Yeah, she *really* won't be down with that. You know how she's gotten now that, we're, you know."

"Together?"

"Yeah."

"Let me talk to her."

"If you insist." I hand my phone to Gran, who's rocking a leopard-print gym suit. I don't know where she finds her outfits.

Zoe confirms that the Brockton Public website has, indeed, announced a cancellation for tomorrow, and I fill them in about Jace's invite to Wes's. "Anyone wanna come?" My teammates aren't really into the Jace Wilder/Wes Jamison party scene. But it'd sure make things easier for me if they started to mingle more. I'd have my own little group to back me up when dealing with Jace's fan club.

"Yeah, right," Zoe says. "Like my dad would let me go to a coed sleepover party, especially one at Wesley Jamison's house." Zoe's dad's a cop and is pretty strict. Not to mention he had some intel about Wes's drug involvement and was not so thrilled the last time he found out we'd been hanging out at Wes's house.

"Boooooooo," I respond. "Gran probably won't be down with me going anyway now that, well..." The guys are watching me, waiting for me to finish my sentence. They weren't at the party last night and, since they aren't exactly part of that crowd, wouldn't have heard about Jace and me yet. "Jace and I are, you know, together now," I tell them.

Charlie doesn't change his expression – and it doesn't surprise me that Zoe spilled the beans to him already – but Rollie and Omar look shocked.

"Are you serious?" Rollie asks.

"Uh, yeah."

"What? It's not that surprising, really," Omar says, masking his disbelief. "I play baseball with the guy and he's always been, like, extra cool with me because Pepper's my friend. And everyone on the team just seems to get you don't talk about Pepper like you talk about other girls. At least not around Wilder."

I let the guys digest the news while I try to eavesdrop on Gran's conversation. I get that Jace Wilder seems untouchable to them, like he still is to Zoe, and that I'm just their teammate and buddy. But still, the looks on their faces! Is it so hard to believe Jace wants to be with me?

Gran hands me the phone before giving me a chance to listen in. "Gran, you need to push the red button when the call is over."

She waves her hand. "I don't know how to work those silly things. The regular telephone works just fine."

"So what's the verdict?" I ask her.

"You can go, and you can stay, but no shenanigans. I'm only letting you stay because it's already late and the roads are going to get worse."

I don't want Gran to know how excited I am about this news so I feign indifference. "Who else wants to come?" I ask the guys.

"I'm down," Omar says. He actually hangs out sometimes with Jace's friends, since they're on the baseball team together. "Rollie?" he asks.

Rollie's eyebrows are scrunched up and I can tell he's conflicted. He's curious to check out the scene, but is hesitant for obvious reasons. We've heard the rumors about how crazy parties hosted by the likes of Wesley Jamison can get. And long-distance runners aren't known for being crazy. At least, not *that* kind of crazy. But Rollie bobs his head after a short contemplation, his red hair falling into his face. Rollie comes from money, so he at least won't feel out of place in the Jamison mansion.

"I'm just going to call it an early night." Charlie tugs Zoe closer to him with his arm around her shoulder. "I've got a research paper I should work on tomorrow anyway, so I don't want to be up all night."

"Awww, you're such a good boyfriend, Charles." Zoe rubs his head full of curly blonde locks. "You just don't want to ditch me."

Charlie smiles sheepishly.

I stuff some sleep clothes and a toothbrush into a backpack and bundle myself into my down jacket, hat, scarf and mittens. Remembering Wes's hot tub, I throw a bikini in my bag before heading out the door.

Rollie's got some big SUV that looks like it will handle the snow and I hop into the back, letting Omar take the front. Zoe waves goodbye as she pulls out with Charlie in the passenger seat. Good boyfriend? Sure. But he is totally using this opportunity to get some alone time with Zoe.

"Who all is going to be there?" Rollie asks. "Is it, like, a Lincoln party, or will there be Public people there too?" He pushes his glasses up on his nose, a nervous gesture of his.

"No idea, Rolls. Sounded like just Wes and Jace were there a few minutes ago."

"Wesley doesn't play a winter sport either, right?" Omar asks.

"Nope. Jace and Wes always just played football and baseball." And they're both really good. Though Jace is better.

"Where's Wes going to college?" Omar asks. "I know Jace signed with UC, which totally rocks. He might get to start there as a freshman. Their QB really hasn't pulled through the past couple years."

"No idea where Wes is going." His dad wants him to go to his alma mater, Princeton. Although not as good as Jace, Wes would be able to play football at an Ivy. I think he actually does pretty well in school too, despite his partying ways.

But Wes applied to a bunch of other colleges too. He knows he'll only get accepted to Princeton because of his dad, and I think he wants to do his own thing. The two have never been close.

Wes likes his privacy just like Jace, so I refrain from unloading the entire explanation on Omar and Rollie, who have moved on to talking about college football.

Glancing out the window, I reflect on my relationship with Wes. I've spent more time with him the past couple of months than I had throughout high school. Jace, Wes and I were inseparable until Wes and Jace started their freshman year at different schools. They had some sort of falling-out that I never got the details on, but apparently reconciled this past year... as drug dealing partners. That's all over now though, and they've started hanging together a lot more. As friends. Wes was the first to know about Jace and me. He didn't act the least bit surprised when we told him, and actually told us "it was about time." I felt the same way.

Chapter 5

When we pull up to the Jamisons', there are only a few cars in the driveway.

"Whoa, this place is even crazier than yours, Rollie," Omar exclaims as he jumps out.

We wander inside. "Hello?" I call out.

"Hey Pepper!" Wes shouts from the kitchen.

Jace shuffles into the entryway. My eyes immediately take in his low-riding jeans that hug his butt and a thermal shirt that makes it look like his pecs and biceps will burst through.

"Are you wearing Wes's clothes?" I ask. Jace doesn't usually sport tight clothing. He doesn't need to show off his assets.

"Yeah, we came right here after the gym and I didn't have any clothes to change into. What do you think?" He smirks at me while he turns around in a circle, having caught me checking him out.

"Oh, I suppose you look okay," I say indifferently, but with a little grin that I can't suppress.

"Lookin' pretty fine yourself, Pep." Jace pulls me in between his legs, and I let him nuzzle my neck for a second before remembering Omar and Rollie.

"Sorry guys," I tell them as I step away from Jace. "You know Omar," I tell Jace. "Have you met Rollie?"

"What's up, man?" Jace asks in greeting.

"Thanks for having us," Rollie says quietly with a shuffle of his feet.

Jace leads us into the kitchen, where Wes is mixing drinks at the counter island. He leans in for a hug and I introduce him to Omar and Rollie.

"I thought you guys were having people over?" I ask.

"I just texted Remy a second ago. I'm sure he'll spread the word." That's how easy it is for a guy like Jace to get a party started. One text message.

I wait to see if Wes will say anything about Madeline coming over, but he's fixated on the liquor bottles lined up in front of him.

"Are Lincoln people coming too?" I don't know how these things work, and I want to be prepared for another confrontation.

"I didn't call anyone," Wes tells me. "Lincoln people might still head over at some point, but I'm hoping to hang with the Brockton Public crowd for a change. Madeline was with me last night, and I could use a break from her."

I frown at him. A break from Madeline Brescoll? "Seriously? Isn't she the hottest girl in this town?" I can't help but ask. It's just my friends here. I can be candid.

Wes gives me a once-over. "She's got plenty of competition for that title."

I roll my eyes. He's just teasing. Right?

I'll never be in Madeline's league, but these *are* my most flattering jeans. Dark-washed and skin-tight all the way to the ankles, I always feel kind of hot when I wear them. They even make it look like I have some curve to my butt and hips. I should start calling them my magical pants.

Wes hands me a drink just as the doorbell rings. He heads to the front door. Rollie and Omar haven't said anything yet. "Do either of you guys want this?" I hold out my drink. "Hard alcohol is not for me."

Omar takes it happily and Jace heads to the fridge. "Beer or wine?"

"I've never tried white wine," I say. I tried red, and didn't like it. And I'm not crazy about beer either. Look at me. Drinking for a second night in a row.

"His mom has this sweet stuff you might like," Jace pulls a bottle of wine out of the fridge and pours me some in a real wine glass.

"Fancy," I remark.

"Only for you, Pep," Jace says with a wink. He turns to Rollie, who is trying unsuccessfully to look casual sitting on a kitchen stool.

"You want a beer, Fowler, or you gonna mix something?"

"You know my last name?" he asks, startled.

"I've lived in this town my whole life. Of course I know the Fowler family. Plus I keep track of Pep's friends," he responds with a grin.

"Creep," I mutter loud enough for him to hear. He only grins wider.

"Beer's great, thanks." Rollie pushes his glasses up on his nose. He likely has no idea how to mix a drink and I could see it going very badly. Beer's a smart choice.

An hour later, the house is packed, and I'm sure I'll never squeeze my way out of the kitchen. But I'm happy in my spot between

Jace's legs. And the wine is actually quite yummy. I'm still nursing the first glass.

Ryan showed up with Remy and Connor, and I wondered how it worked out that Ryan and Jace share friends. It's so strange to me.

Ryan said hello briefly, and then went somewhere with Omar and Rollie, who were thankful to have another friend at the party. But is Ryan really our friend? Since team practices stopped, we'd all stopped hanging out with him. But was that because we broke up? Or is he one of those teammates who only hangs out when it's convenient during the season? Time will tell, I suppose.

Jace is being especially affectionate, kissing my shoulder or forehead every few minutes as he chats with people, and keeping me firmly at his side. I'm not really paying much attention to the people who keep coming up to talk to him. I prefer to take in the scene, people watching. This is all still pretty new to me, and I find it fascinating.

Madeline and her entourage haven't showed up yet. At least, I don't think they have. Most people come to the kitchen first, presumably to get a drink, but I imagine Jace's presence has something to do with it, too. Though the queen bees of Lincoln haven't made an appearance, their equivalents at Brockton Public – labeled the Barbies by Zoe – were some of the first to arrive.

From a few minutes observing, it looks like Kayla Chambers – the ringleader – is hooking up with Jace's best guy friend Remy. Andrea Hill has always been on and off with Connor, Jace's football co-captain. And apparently Lisa is now with Ryan. It's a relief that none of them are gunning for Jace, but just the fact that they have all been with him in the past is enough to get me worked up.

Ben Hughes was apparently seeing Tina Anderson, one of the Barbies in my class, at one point (according to my gossip source, Zoe) but I haven't seen either of them around to confirm.

All the drama never interested me before, but now that I'm Jace's girlfriend, and he is who he is, I can't stay totally oblivious. So far, Madeline Brescoll seems to be the only threat.

Wes's buddies from Lincoln Academy, Forbes Townsend and Pierce Malone, enter the kitchen to whoops of greeting. Though it's mostly Brockton Public people here at this point, everyone knows these two matter.

I stiffen with the realization that their presence means the queen bees will be arriving soon. "What's up?" Jace whispers in my ear.

The feel of his warm breath on my skin distracts me, and I squirm against him in response. My back is to his front, and he tightens his hold around my waist. "Pepper," he says in warning. His voice is gruff, and I love knowing I have some power over him. Because he certainly has some over me.

I take the last sip of my wine, and Jace passes my empty glass to someone. My head leans back against his shoulder as I press harder against him. I feel him against my lower back and my eyes start to drift closed just as he growls and tugs me away toward the stairs.

"You can't tease me like that with all those people around." He almost sounds angry, but I know he isn't. Jace's angry voice is unmistakable. He's only frustrated because he lost a little control. I smile to myself as I follow him upstairs, but I pause when I hear Serena's and Emma's voices. I glance down and see them entering the kitchen, with Madeline in front. Had Jace seen her? Was that why he pulled me away? Or was he overtaken by lust, like I was?

"Hey, lovebirds!" Wes calls to us from upstairs. "Come on out to the hot tub! We can watch the storm." He walks down the hallway in a bathing suit and flip flops. His body type is similar to Jace's – lean and muscular – but Jace has broader shoulders and is a little taller.

I laugh. "Oh please, you'll have plenty of girls following you out there if you walk through the house like that."

Jace pulls me to him, letting me know he didn't really appreciate that comment. Yeah, that was probably inappropriate. Oops.

Wes just chuckles. "I'll save you space."

Wes slides down the banister, just like I saw him do a million times when we were kids. Still, it makes my heart race every time, knowing he could fall and break his neck.

"That actually sounds awesome. Hot tub in a blizzard? Let's change." Jace goes straight to a drawer in Wes's room and pulls out two sets of swim trunks. "You got a sports bra?" he asks, tossing me boys' swim trunks.

"Even better, I've got a bikini," I say with a smile, thankful I threw one in at the last minute.

When I come out of the bathroom a few minutes later in my polka-dotted string bikini, Jace takes one look at me and rubs his hand over his face. "You need to wear those shorts out to the pool." He picks up the swim trunks I left on the floor and hands them to me.

Rolling my eyes, I pull the trunks on. I don't exactly want to strut through the house in a bikini anyway.

I peek through the screen before going outside. I want to run immediately into the hot tub without freezing my butt off any longer than possible. But the tub is full.

"I told him that would happen!" I huff out.

Jace grins and looks out the door. He catches Wes's attention and in the next minute, two girls come inside dripping wet. "There's space now," they announce, not even sounding annoyed that they were just kicked out.

Ah, to be Jace Wilder.

I'm surprised to see Omar, Rollie and Ryan in the tub with Wes. There are also two girls on either side of Wes whom I don't know. And Lisa is leaning against Ryan. Good thing I'd learned about them earlier that day so I'm able to keep a blank expression.

Jace eases in behind me and arranges himself along a headrest with his feet out before pulling me onto his lap. We have the clutch seat – the one that's shaped for lying down with a curve and a head rest.

The snow is dumping all around us, and I immediately feel some gather on my cheeks and eyelashes.

"So what's your plan for track this season, Pep?" Wes asks.

I shrug. I haven't given track season much thought. I was so wound up for Nationals that when cross season ended, I didn't want to think about what was next. Plus, I've been consumed with Jace these past couple of months. "Just the usual, probably. I'll run the mile and 2-mile at State, and hopefully we'll have a distance medley relay."

"Carrie and Lauren here run track," Wes informs me. I squint through the steam, trying to place them.

"Cool, what events?"

"Same as you," Lauren says.

"We do cross too, but you know, we don't really race Brockton Public," the one named Carrie explains.

"We thought you'd go for Nationals in track this year since you won Nationals in cross. Plus they have the 5k at Nationals, and you're better at longer distances," Lauren tells me.

I shift in Jace's lap. I'm still getting used to the idea that strangers talk about my running.

"Nationals will probably be a last-minute decision for us," Ryan speaks up. "Track season is so long as it is, and there's tons of competition in Colorado, so track Nationals isn't as big a thing."

Oh. I didn't know that.

"Yeah, plus aren't there like two big national meets and the best people aren't at both of them? Kind of kills the idea of a national meet," Carrie adds.

I didn't know that either. I actually have no idea what the qualifying times are for my events.

"You should look into the records, Pep," Omar says. "I bet you could go for one of them."

Does he mean state or national records?

"I don't want to think about it yet. I'm still winding down from cross season," I announce. My good mood – from the wine, hot tub, cookies, and the snow day – quickly fizzles at the mention of track season.

Until this conversation, I didn't realize how much I've been avoiding thinking about competition. I haven't been avoiding thinking about running, because I love to run and do it nearly every day. But I'm not ready to think about times, races, and goals. Cross took more out of me mentally than I realized. I was so focused, and now I just want to have some fun.

The conversation moves on to baseball, but I feel Ryan's gaze on me.

Is that all it is? Wanting to be a normal teenager? Does the pressure of winning really get to me that much? Am I burning out already? A cold fear takes hold of me, and I shiver despite the hot water. After winning Nationals, there's nowhere for me to go but down.

Chapter 6

By the time we get out of the hot tub, everyone seems to be a bit drunk except for me, Jace and Ryan. I watch the others stumble inside as I lift the hot tub cover.

"We got this, Pep," Wes says, taking the cover from me.

Jace grabs the other side of the cover and I head inside. As I close the sliding glass door, I hear Wes say angrily, "What the hell, man? I thought you were going to tell her! We just talked about it."

"Not when people are over. Now's not the time," Jace says sternly.

"That's why you invited people over, isn't it?" Wes asks.

"Dude, we always party when there's a snow day. I'll talk to her tomorrow morning after everyone leaves."

Jace has a knack for responding to questions he doesn't want to answer, without actually answering the question.

"People aren't going to leave. It's a snow day. That's the point."

"They will if we tell them to. Besides, what's the rush? It's been years. One more day won't hurt."

"Your mom's back now, Jace."

A deep unease settles over me. I can't even begin to imagine what it is they're talking about. And what does Jace's mom being back have anything to do with it?

I hear them making their way to the door and I pretend to be engrossed in drying myself off. Should I ask what they were talking about? Or wait until tomorrow?

The decision is made for me when Carrie and Lauren call Wes over, and he heads off with them. Has Wes always been such a slut? I frown, realizing I have no idea. He was with Madeline last night and now two new girls. That's a lot of action. Maybe all the popular guys are like that.

I see Ryan heading upstairs with Lisa and my frown deepens. Even Ryan went from his ex-girlfriend, Kate, in California, to me pretty quickly. And now Lisa.

"I'm ready for bed," Jace tells me after drying off.

"First I want another glass of that white wine." I walk up the stairs without a glance in Jace's direction. Based on the tone of his voice, I know he's giving me a look that says he wants to go to bed, but not to sleep. But I can't look at him right now. I don't feel entirely justified in being angry, since I have no idea what the secret is that they've kept from me. Still, just the thought they've kept any kind of secret for this long is deeply disturbing.

As I make my way to the fridge, the feel of gazes weighs on me, and I realize I didn't put the swim trunks back on or grab a towel. I'm just strutting my stuff, Madeline Brescoll-style. Groaning inwardly, I open the fridge door, wishing I could hide inside it. I immediately spot the bottle of wine I was drinking earlier because someone taped a label to it that says "Pepper's wine". How did *that* happen?

Shutting the door, I turn to reach in the cupboard for a wine glass but am blocked by a firm, wet chest. Jace holds out an empty glass with his eyebrows raised.

As I pour myself a generous cup, he wraps a towel over my shoulders. Even without it, I already feel less exposed with him behind me, blocking the view.

He takes me upstairs to one of the guest rooms and turns on the shower. I lean against the door, and we watch each other in the mirror.

"Are we going to take a shower together?" I ask. We've never been naked together before. This would be... huge. I gulp the wine.

Jace's eyes darken. "Do you want to?"

I nod. My emotions are a mess right now. From Jace's mom, to track season apprehension, to whatever secret the boys are keeping from me. But watching Jace in his swim trunks, his jet black hair wet and tousled and those eyes boring into mine, all I really want right now is him.

"Bathing suits on or off?" His voice sounds hoarse.

I take another gulp of wine and place it on the bathroom counter before untying the back of my swimsuit and letting it fall to the floor. My back is to him but he can see me in the mirror. He moves closer as I reach for my bottoms. "I'll do it," he whispers. He pulls them slowly down my legs, and the heat from his hands leaves tingles. I step out of my suit and see myself completely naked in the mirror.

Jace's hands roam back up my legs, over my hips and stomach, and cup my breasts. He lets out a shaky breath before pulling my hair to the side and nuzzling my neck. Of all my body parts, it must be my neck he loves the most. He's always putting his face there to breathe me in and kiss me. Or maybe he just knows how much it affects me.

I sink into him, feeling him through his bathing suit. Moaning as he massages my breasts in his palms, I reach behind me and tug on the waistband of his suit. He lets out a chuckle.

I turn around and tug the shorts down, watching in fascination as he springs free. Just like last night, I can't hide my shock. It's just too much. His shorts drop to the ground and he steps out of them. Without thinking, my hands reach for him, and wrap around the thick length.

He lets out a groan and his eyelids fall closed. "I thought we were taking a shower." I hardly recognize his voice, and I grin at the power I have over him right now.

He walks backwards toward the shower, and my hands slip. I follow him in and lean my head back under the showerhead. It's a huge shower with glass doors and a granite bench.

Jace watches me as he runs a bar of soap over his body.

"What was bothering you?" he asks.

I pour some shampoo into my hand, wondering how to respond. I can't concentrate right now. When I start to scrub it through my hair, Jace begins to run the soap over my stomach and legs, and then I really lose all ability to think clearly.

"Jace." My voice is needy.

"What had you upset, Pep?"

He stops soaping me and turns the full force of his eyes to mine.

I sigh. "I don't feel like talking about it." I can't lie to this boy. He knows me too well.

"Was it running? You can talk to me about it, Pep."

"That's part of it, yeah. But really, I'll sort it out." He looks hurt that I'm not opening up, but he does the same thing to me all the time. "Just make me feel better for now?"

He shakes his head, but resumes soaping me as I rinse the shampoo out of my hair.

We don't say anything when we step out of the shower, or when he dries me off with a towel.

"That was the best shower I've ever had," Jace announces.

"You haven't even kissed me yet," I say with a pout.

Jace lifts my chin and takes my mouth in his. His tongue slips inside as he lets the towel drop between us. This is dangerous. We are completely naked. And it sends a thrill through me. I take a step closer. I can feel his body an inch from mine, but we aren't touching.

He pulls away. We are both breathing heavily.

"Let's put some clothes on," he says through a ragged breath.

"Jace. Why?" I want his tongue in my mouth again. And his body against mine.

He raises his eyes to look at me.

"I want you. You obviously want me. Why are you putting on the brakes?" I ask. My body is on fire. I'm ready for this. And I've always wanted Jace to be the one. We have our own bed and everything.

Jace shakes his head. "You've been drinking, and you were upset about something that you won't talk to me about. And we're at a party. It's not right."

"Not right for whom?" I ask. This is the same conversation we had last night, but I need more of an explanation.

Jace's face suddenly takes on a pained expression, and he steps back. "Wait. This

would be your first time, right? You didn't –"
He stutters. "With –" He can't finish. I've never
seen him this shaken.

I shake my head quickly to put him out of his
misery. "No."

His expression immediately relaxes.

"But Jace, you've done it a lot. With a lot of
different people. So if I'm ready, what's the
problem?"

Jace takes a bathrobe off of a hook and hands
it to me. He walks into the bedroom and pulls
on a pair of sweat pants. "Put that on." He
points to the robe in my hand and I let out an
exaggerated sigh as I comply.

"It's a big deal for me to sleep with you, Pep,
even though I've slept with other people," he
says as he makes his way to the bed and lies
down on his back. He pats the spot next to
him and I curl up at his side. "There's no rush.
I'm so fucking happy to be with you. To be
your boyfriend. Hell, of course I want you. But
we should wait for a better time. When there's
nothing else between us."

I sit up to look at him. "What's between us?"

He clenches his jaw. My heart starts to race.
The secret. "Nothing between *us*," he forces
out. "I just meant, we only let people know

about us yesterday, my mom showed up this morning, and you've got something on your mind about running, or whatever it is you won't talk about..."

I stare at him. So he isn't going to tell me. Yet. I'll wait until tomorrow. And if he doesn't say anything, I'll force it out of him.

***

I wake to a pillow being thrown in my face. "Huh?" I peek out from under the covers to see Wes standing over the bed wearing nothing but flannel pajama bottoms and a goofy grin.

"Rise and shine, sleepyheads!" he says with way too much enthusiasm.

I throw the pillow back at him, and he uses it to beat Jace over the head. A muffled growl is the only response.

"What time is it? And why aren't you ever wearing a shirt?" I ask as I sit up and brush the hair out of my face.

"I could ask you the same," Wes says with a smirk.

I glance down. A blanket covers the essentials, but I must have kicked off the bathrobe I'd fallen asleep in at some point during the night.

Jace leans up on an elbow and glares at Wes. "Get outta here, man," he says grumpily.

"No way. The three of us are going out to breakfast. I'm too hung over to sleep. And I'm not fixing something to eat here. Everyone will want some."

"How many people are still here?" I ask, pulling the bedcover up to cover my shoulders.

Wes shrugs. "Looks like everyone stayed. It's still storming out there, too, so who knows when people will get outta here. Let's go to Hal's. I need something greasy."

Hal's Diner certainly knows how to do greasy.

"What? Are we taking a snowmobile?" I ask with a frown.

Wes laughs and Jace lets out some sort of grunt as he buries himself deeper into his pillow.

"There's a Hummer in the garage. It'll drive in anything."

Wes lingers in the room and opens the shades to let in some light.

"Are you gonna get outta here so we can change or what?" I ask.

"You'll just go back to sleep. I need to supervise and make sure you get up."

"Jeez, you're persistent." If I hadn't heard the conversation last night, I'd be pretty confused about Wes's eagerness to get breakfast. Especially when I have no doubt there's plenty of others he could recruit in our place to accompany him. "We'll meet you downstairs in ten minutes."

Wes eyes me skeptically but I stare him down with enough authority that he leaves our room a moment later.

There are two approaches I can take to waking Jace, who's never been a morning person. Before he became my boyfriend, I'd shove him and annoy him into waking up. I'd get an awake Jace, but a grumpy one. However, now that I'm his girlfriend...

I snuggle up close to his warm body and start kissing his back, making my way up his shoulders and neck. I can feel his smile as my lips make their way to his mouth.

"Morning," I whisper. My hands slide down his back and along the band of his boxer briefs. Jace pulls me to him and nestles his head in my neck.

His hands roam around the sheet I'm wrapped up in. "Are you naked underneath this?" he asks gruffly.

"Maybe," I say with a smile.

In one quick movement, Jace flips from his stomach to his back, and rolls me on top of him.

He's awake now, that's for sure.

Jace brushes the hair out of my face before giving me a scorching kiss. But even as I feel him stir beneath me, he pulls away. I'm getting used to it.

"So I heard something about Hal's?" he asks.

"We're meeting Wes downstairs in five minutes."

Jace sits up and I wrap my legs around his waist before he stands and walks us into the bathroom. The sheet is still around me as we brush our teeth, glancing at each other every few seconds with goofy grins. We haven't woken up together like this before, and I'm not sure I'll ever want to wake up alone again.

I feel amazing this morning, even having gone to bed upset. Maybe it's because I know that I'll find out whatever they've been keeping from me today. Or maybe it's the blizzard outside. Snowy days always make me feel warm and cozy. But I'm pretty sure it's simply that Jace is here, right next to me, and he's mine.

His dark hair's been styled in a faux hawk for so long now that it falls into a sexy mess without any effort on his part. Jace's olive skin maintains a glow throughout the year, even when his summer tan has faded. I watch his back muscles flex as he reaches down to pick jeans up from the floor and pull them on.

He catches me watching and gives me one of his smiles that make me melt. Every. Time.

"Get your clothes on, Pep. I don't want Wes barging in here and seeing you naked."

Ten minutes later we drive down an empty main street. The piles of snow along the sidewalk indicate that the roads were plowed at some point that morning, but with the snow still falling, they remain slick.

A few folks sit at the counter when we enter Hal's Diner, but the place isn't packed like most mornings. We slide into a booth and the boys order coffee while I get an orange juice.

No one says anything as we sip our drinks. We all look out the window, watching the snow fall. If I didn't know better, I might mistake it for a comfortable silence.

When the food arrives – we all ordered the $4.99 special of two eggs, bacon, toast, and a pancake – I catch Wes and Jace in some sort of silent exchange. It's what we used to order years ago when Jim would take the three of us here. I could never finish mine back then, and if I wasn't so wound up with curiosity this morning, I'd probably scarf the whole thing down in minutes.

As I pour an excessive amount of syrup over the bacon and pancake, Wes clears his throat. "So, Pep. We wanted to –"

He's cut off by Jace. "Wes. Shut up." It's a calm and controlled command, but I know that tone. He's not to be messed with right now.

Jace turns to face me.

"There's not an easy way to break this to you, Pep, so I'm just gonna say it."

He pauses. I stare at him, waiting. Jace's jaw clenches but he doesn't break eye contact with me.

"Me and Wes. We're brothers."

Chapter 7

I put my fork down and clasp my hands in my lap. I have to look away.

My heart is beating so fast, I'm sure everyone can hear it.

"Have you always known?" I finally ask. My gaze focuses on the snowflakes sliding down the window.

Jace answers, "We found out the summer before we started high school."

I whip my head around and look between them. "Why didn't you tell me? The three of us... we were best friends. Why would you keep this from me?" I don't hide the pain in my voice. This hurts. They are family? *Real* family. They both have a sibling – each other. And me? I have no siblings. No parents.

Jace nods at Wes, who shifts forward in his seat. "Jim told us. He's our dad. He said he always wanted us to know, but my mom didn't want that. My mom and dad – well, David, I guess – have never had a normal marriage. I think they've always slept with other people," he says with a shrug. "But that's just the way it's been since I can remember."

I nod slowly. There are so many questions, but I can tell Wes has been waiting a long time to let it all out, and I don't want to interrupt.

"At first, I was so angry. And I took it out on Jace. You would think I'd be psyched to have a brother. But I blamed Jim and Jace, and my mom, for the way my dad – David – treated me. You know, he's never around. He just wants me to be a kid with enough achievements that I'm not an embarrassment. Someone he can talk about when asked by his buddies. He's never really cared about me."

Wes's face is full of emotion, and I'm shocked that he's telling me all this. We only recently started hanging out again. And these are some deep feelings he's revealing. With no restraint. I can't help but feel closer to him. Like the four years without him in my life never happened.

He sighs and runs his hand through his hair. The same way Jace does when he's thinking. How had I not recognized this before? I guess I *had* noticed similarities, but it never occurred to me it might be because they are related.

"Anyway, it's hard to explain. But I was angry. I was only 14."

"You were angry? That's why no one told me?" My voice is soft, because I know this isn't easy for Wes. But now I'm the one who's angry.

Although it's directed mostly at Jace. He should have told me. He and I have stayed friends all these years, and he never said a thing.

My gaze turns to him and I can see the regret in his eyes.

"We should have told you, Pep. You've been our friend our whole lives."

"I'm not going to forgive you so quickly. What's *your* excuse?"

Jace looks down into his coffee mug. "I was angry too. It's hard to explain why. I always wanted to blame someone for my mom leaving. It wasn't Wes's fault. Obviously. But he represented something, you know? All the shitty feelings I never knew I had from my mom leaving rose to the surface. Wes still had two parents, and that pissed me off. I didn't want anything to do with Wes anymore."

I study Jace's expression. He's being honest. More honest about his feelings on this than he's ever been before. But there's more to it. I can tell by the way his jaw twitches just a bit.

I go with my gut and decide now's not the time to push it.

He clears his throat and continues, "Now I've realized that my dad's affair probably didn't have anything to do with my mom leaving."

That gets my attention. And Wes's too, judging by the way he stiffens across the table.

"My mom called me a few months ago. My dad never talked about it because I never asked, but I knew they had never been married. She was only 21 when I was born, and in college still. Even once my mom found out she was pregnant, I don't think they talked about getting married. So, I had to admit to myself that the affair didn't have anything to do with her leaving. I mean, she didn't leave until a few years later, and she knew about Wes when he was born a couple months after me."

I hear the pain in his voice for a second but he quickly masks it.

"She called to tell me she was going to be leaving rehab soon, and she wanted to meet me. Annie was an addict when she left, and has been on and off since."

Wes and I wait for Jace to continue, but when he takes another sip of coffee and looks up, it's clear he's done. That's all we're going to get.

"And now she's here. Isn't it Annie you should be angry with?" I ask what seems to me to be the logical question.

Jace's eyes narrow. "She wasn't much older than us when she got pregnant with me, and she had a lot of her own problems. She wasn't in the kind of shape she needed to be to be a mom."

I gape at him, and I sense Wes shifting uncomfortably, probably trying to suppress his response. Jace is defending her. Protecting her. I shake my head. It makes no sense.

Jace bites into a piece of bacon and the conversation's over.

My head spins as I pick at my eggs. My appetite has vanished, and I let the boys finish off my breakfast.

"Party's still going on at my place. You guys coming?" Wes asks when we get back in the Hummer.

"Not me. I'm going for a run."

Even though I wasn't planning on running today, the urge to lace up and get outside is overwhelming.

"Seriously? In this weather?" Wes gives me a hard look in the rearview mirror.

I shrug.

When we pull up to my apartment, Jace says he's going back to Wes's and will get my sleepover bag that I left behind. He's used to me running in all kinds of weather. "Call me after your run."

I nod and wave goodbye.

Gran is chatting with her BFF Lulu in the living room when I get home. Hanson's Christmas music plays quietly in the background.

"Tell us all about the sleepover party!" Gran exclaims.

"Did anything scandalous happen?" Lulu asks with a gleam in her eye.

Despite the turmoil ripping through my body, I smile. "Sorry ladies, no gossip for you," I say with a shake of my finger. "I'm going for a run."

Gran protests against me going out in the storm, but eventually gives up, insisting that I take my cell phone. "I guess it does have its uses," she admits.

Before Dave and I head out, Gran inspects my clothing, making sure I'm wearing enough layers. I'm halfway down the stairwell when I pause and gasp. Dave perks his ears up and gives me a quizzical look.

I rush back up the stairs and open the door to our apartment.

"You knew, didn't you?" I ask Gran. She's in the kitchen, pouring coffee into a mug. Lulu can hear us from the living room, but I don't care.

Gran turns to me. "Knew what?"

Of course, she wouldn't know that I just found out. After all these years.

"Jace and Wes. They just told me." The understanding in her eyes is immediate, and it answers my question even without the nod.

"Yes, I've known most of your life. But it's never been for me to share."

The pain I felt when they first told me slices through me again. They all knew. Except for me. I was left out.

"I'm going for a run," I force out.

***

The blizzard echoes the whirlwind of emotions swirling inside of me. Wind sends snow hurling at me in gusts, and I welcome the snowy terrain. I focus on keeping my footing and it provides the distraction I'm seeking. I don't want to dissect the myriad of feelings coursing through me right now. They don't make any sense and I don't understand where they are coming from.

So what if Wes and Jace are brothers? Why does it matter that I'm only hearing about it now when even Gran has known all along?

Because they are your family. *Your only family,* an angry little voice in my head shouts.

My thoughts flash to a memory of a picture I drew in elementary school. We were told to draw a picture of our family, but I was the only one with just one person – Gran – and I didn't like it. So I included Wes and Jace, and told the teacher they were my brothers. Obviously, I don't think of Jace as my sibling anymore, but even at seven or eight years old I understood that those boys would be there for me like family.

Except I lost Wes because no one would tell me what was going on. Now he and Jace are family again. And me? What am I? Jace's girlfriend. And what does Wes want?

I pick up my speed and Dave looks up at me, eager for the challenge. The blizzard isn't enough of a distraction after all, and I seek out a burn in my legs and lungs to take away the ache in my chest.

Over an hour later, I'm thoroughly numb emotionally, and burning up from physical exertion. I'm also at a point along the bike path I don't recognize. Even if I turn around now, it will be the longest run I've ever been on. And I must have left my phone on the kitchen counter because I'm only now realizing it's not in my jacket pocket.

I pause for a moment on the path while Dave takes a sip of water from the creek. The snow is letting up, but the wind is getting stronger. I haven't seen a single other person on the path yet, and as my body temperature starts to drop, I realize I may have overdone it.

The wind was howling on the way out, but apparently it was at my back most of the time. As I head in the opposite direction, I'm nearly knocked over with the strength of it directly hitting my chest. I ran hard on the way out, and I can't maintain that effort the rest of the way. It's going to take me a while to get back, and I hope Gran doesn't freak out.

Another hour later, and I've reached one of my usual turn around points. I figure I ran nearly 10 miles out, and I'm still several miles from home. If I've run as far as I expect, that's at least a half marathon. In a blizzard. My long runs are typically 70-90 minutes... and not in the snow. I've been out for over two hours.

The wind is head-on, and my legs are trashed. But at least the only thing I'm feeling right now is fatigue. And there's a mild panic beginning to seep through me as my legs protest forward movement.

I slow to a walk. Just for a few minutes, to rest. My muscles feel like bricks. Heavy. Even Dave looks ready to quit, and that dog's like the Energizer Bunny.

My face is raw from the wind. The sweat I generated during the beginning of the run is now making me shiver. It takes all my focus to lift each foot and place it in front of me. Is that pain in my stomach hunger? The two bites of eggs this morning definitely did not provide the kind of fuel I needed.

I see a figure jogging toward me. Who else is crazy enough to be running in this weather? The wind is brutal. I have to lean forward to avoid getting knocked over.

"Pepper?" I hear Ryan's voice call out. "Are you okay?" He picks up his pace. Jeez, do I really look that terrible? I guess it's strange to him that I'm not running.

He reaches me and puts his hands on my shoulders. "You're weaving a little. What's going on?"

"Do you have a phone on you? My Gran is probably freaking out."

"I don't. Let's walk back to my house and we'll call her. It's closer."

He puts his arm around me and I lean in, thankful for the extra protection from the wind. It seems to be getting stronger but maybe I'm getting weaker.

"Talk to me. How long were you running?"

I check my watch. "I guess I've been out for almost two and a half hours, but I stopped running a few minutes ago. I was at the railroad tracks when I turned around." My voice cracks from the dryness in my throat. Despite freezing temperatures, I'm parched.

"The railroad in Dryden? What were you doing all the way out there?"

"I don't know. I just kept running."

Ryan doesn't respond for a moment. He must think I'm nuts. Maybe I am.

"Does this have anything to do with what those girls were saying last night? You know you don't have to prove anything, Pep. Just because you won Nationals doesn't mean you have to start training like a maniac in order to meet other people's expectations."

Is that why I did it? No, that has nothing to do with it. He wouldn't understand. And I can't tell him anyway. Heck, no one told me until this morning. And I'm supposed to be family! My blood boils even through the fatigue. Running can only suppress the emotions for so long.

"No, I wasn't even thinking about that. I actually haven't thought much about track at all. I just..." It's so easy to open up with Ryan. He really seems to want to listen. But no, I can't go there. "I just felt like running," I say quietly. "Why are you out in this weather?" I turn the questioning on him.

"I don't exactly get much of a workout running with Lisa. And that was my only run yesterday."

Ah, that's right. Lisa.

Two other figures are walking our way. And even through my frozen eyelashes, I recognize them. Same confident stride. How did I not see it before?

"Is that Jace? And Wesley?" Ryan asks as we get closer.

"Gran must have sent them out to get me." Oh, joy. I'm going to get a lecture. From all three of them. Jace, Wes *and* Gran.

I have a feeling Wes is trying to get us back to the threesome we used to be. But that's impossible. He and Jace are real brothers. And Jace is my boyfriend. The balance between the three of us will never be the same again.

When we near them, Jace's green eyes are wild. He looks ready to pounce on Ryan. I step out of Ryan's hold and make my way to Jace. For the brief moment between the two of them, I almost lose my balance. Wow. I really messed myself up.

Jace catches me. "I'm carrying you to the car," he says darkly and scoops me up in his arms.

His chest is warm, and my brain immediately starts shutting down. I'm safe now. I remained coherent, I think, while walking with Ryan. But now, my head is spinning and I can barely process where we are as Jace piles me into the front seat of a pickup truck. It looks like a parking lot but I don't recognize my surroundings with all the snow.

He heads over to the driver's side, turns the truck on and blasts the heat before shutting the door again. I watch him talk to Ryan and Wes. Was this a rescue mission? Oh no!

I throw myself over to the driver's seat and swing the door open in panic. "Dave? Where is he?"

Dave jumps up on the seat and licks my face. I sigh and rest my head against him. But he's pulled away and I hear Wes call Dave into the bed of the truck.

Ryan and Jace are arguing. I can't make out what they're saying over the wind, but I know both of their stances and expressions well enough to process that neither are happy.

I don't want to handle this right now. I'm too tired to care.

Chapter 8

I fall into a half-sleep. Male voices argue, and I'm lifted out of the truck. I let my limbs rest on strong arms. They smell like wood, spice and boy, and my brain registers that Jace and Wes have always shared a similar scent. I don't bother verifying whose arms I'm in because my head is too heavy to lift.

When I settle into my bed, a comforter tucked under my chin, my mind drifts to memories I haven't visited in years.

It was a Friday night and the boys were at my front door. I had on purple flannel pajama bottoms and a tank top, and the boys were in similar cozy attire.

"What are you guys doing here?" I asked. "The dance started twenty minutes ago!" All the eighth-graders had been talking about for the past month was the graduation dance.

The boys barged into the kitchen, throwing popcorn in the microwave and pulling mugs from the cupboard for hot chocolate.

"The dance is stupid, Pep," Jace explained. "There are so many chaperones watching like hawks, it ruins the fun."

"Whatever, man, you wanted to go until I said I was ditching to hang with Pep," Wes said as he punched Jace playfully on the arm.

"So?" Jace said coolly. "There aren't really any girls at the dance I want to make out with anyway. I'm ready for high school."

"You guys can't just skip the dance. It's a big deal! Besides, I'm already planning on watching *Kill Bill* and you guys have seen it a million times."

"So have you!" Wes said, laughing. "I call couch!" he yelled before running out of the kitchen and hurdling over the couch.

I sighed in mock annoyance, but really I couldn't have been happier for their company. Gran was playing Bingo someplace with Lulu, and it could get kind of lonely in the apartment at night.

Jace settled on the ground in front of the couch. He threw my legs over his shoulders and leaned back.

"Dude. Why are you sitting there?" Wes asked as the previews started. "The armchair's free."

Jace shrugged in answer and tossed a handful of popcorn in his mouth. "Maybe I want to cuddle with the family here, and I don't want to be all alone on the chair?" he said while munching away.

Wes's arm was up on the back of the couch, but he dropped it around my shoulder and tugged me closer to him. In contrast to Jace's positioning of my legs, Wes's movements felt more deliberate. I was now quite close to him, my head resting on his shoulder. It would have been intimate if Jace hadn't been sitting with us.

I listened to the boys crack jokes about the previews and shook off the butterflies in my stomach. Wes had always been a cutie, but he'd pulled me in for hugs a million times, and this was no different. I sipped my hot chocolate and smiled, easing into the couch with my two best friends.

My memory floats to four months later, when Wes had answered my phone call with a cold tone.

"The new Jackass movie just came out, and you said you'd go with me, remember?" I asked him.

"I can't go, sorry, Pep. You should ask Jace. He'll go with you." Wes sounded distracted, and not all that happy to hear from me. I'd called him a few times over the last couple weeks, but this was the first time he'd answered.

"He's at an away game all weekend," I told Wes.

"Listen, Pepper, I gotta go," Wes said after an awkward silence. That was it. No explanation as to where he was going, or when we would speak again.

"So, now that you're in high school, you're too cool to hang out with me?" I expected him to deny it, but he just let out a heavy sigh. "Jace still hangs out with me, you know? Is it because you're in private school? We're not good enough for you?" I asked in a teasing tone, although I feared I was hitting on the truth. Why else hadn't I heard from Wesley since school started?

Wes mumbled a response before hanging up, leaving me to conclude that after years of friendship, Wesley had made new friends, and I'd been left behind. And had he moved on from Jace too? Whenever I asked Jace about Wes, I got an evasive response.

I found out later that Wes had shown up for his first day at Lincoln Academy with a black eye. People said that Jace did it, but no one knew why. Jace denied it. I remember hurting a lot that year. From Wesley's rejection, and because Jace wouldn't talk to me about it. That was the beginning of us growing apart. All three of us.

As I fall into a deeper sleep, memories of our years together – and apart – drift between reality and dream. The three of us used to be equals in friendship, but my mind struggles with where I fit in now that I've been let in on their secret.

***

When I wake up, it's dark outside. My legs are stiff as I stumble to the bathroom. The clock says 7:15. I must have slept through the afternoon.

Even though I plan to go straight back to sleep, I find myself brushing my teeth. It's habit. I watch myself in the mirror. Was it only this morning that I was brushing my teeth with Jace? It seems like ages ago.

And when I leave the bathroom, he's waiting for me. Leaning against my bedroom door.

My body doesn't consult my brain or anything else. It just knows it wants Jace's comfort. I walk into his arms and nestle my head into his chest.

He sighs and draws me closer, giving me a kiss on the top of my head.

"I have to go," he tells me.

"You do? Why?" I look up at him, and see his brow furrowed. He's conflicted about something.

"My mom. She called this morning, after breakfast, and before we found you. I'm meeting her for dinner." He tucks a lock of hair behind my ear. "You should eat something. Buns made chicken dumpling soup."

I want to ask Jace more about his mom, but my stomach growls and getting food becomes my first priority.

Jace sits me down at the kitchen table and returns a moment later with a bowl of soup, crackers, and a glass of water. I don't mind being treated like a child right now. I'm still half asleep.

"School again tomorrow. I'll pick you up normal time." Jace leaves another kiss on my head before heading out. As I finish my soup in a daze, Gran shuffles in.

I tense for a lecture, but she doesn't seem inclined to give one.

Instead, she asks if I want dessert. I shake my head. "I'm sorry, Gran. I didn't mean to be out so long and worry you."

She sighs. "I know."

Gran rests her elbows on the table and places her chin on her clasped hands. "So, Jace's mom is back."

Oh. We're having this conversation. "Gran, I'm exhausted. Do we have to talk about this now?"

She shrugs. "I spoke with Jace about it earlier, and I don't want you to feel out of the loop."

My eyes widen. Jace spoke to Gran about his mom, but not me? I suppose she does have a way of getting information out of people when she wants it.

"What did you talk about?"

"He wants a relationship with her. He wants to get to know her."

"I don't get it. How can he forgive her so easily? She abandoned him." I always felt Jace was the way he was – that is, always trying to maintain control of his emotions and relationships – because of what she did to him. But he's acting like she didn't do anything wrong.

"If you want my opinion, he just wants her to love him." Gran sits back in her chair, and I wait for her to explain that statement. But all she adds is, "He thinks he needs her love, her acceptance."

Gran makes it sound so simple. So uncomplicated. It's not though.

"Why? Jace has plenty of love. I love him. You love him. Jim, Wes... the whole town loves that boy."

Gran chuckles. "Well, as far as the town goes – lust and infatuation aren't love – but I know what you're saying." She sobers. "A mother's love is unique though, Pep." She takes my hand. "You had that when Vanessa and Danny were alive. They were taken from you, but you've always known their love couldn't be taken. With Annie, her leaving was like telling Jace she didn't love him. She's been here, on this earth, his whole life. And now that she's in Brockton, Jace wants to earn her approval, and her love." Gran's voice breaks. I don't think I've ever seen her so emotional. It rattles me.

"He shouldn't have to earn his mom's love," I say coldly. "She should be earning his."

"I agree, Pep. I don't like it. Don't like it one bit." Gran sits up and heads over to the liquor cabinet to mix herself a drink. "I don't know how it's going to play out, but that woman was always a selfish one. Sure, she was young and maybe people can grow out of selfishness, but I don't trust her. I worry about Jace. And then I worry about you. Because you and Jace have always gone together. He hurts, you'll hurt."

She stirs her drink, contemplating this. It's all true.

"What should I do?" I ask quietly.

"We can't get in the middle of it. Jace is determined to get to know her."

"Did he tell you that?"

Gran gives me a knowing smile. "Well, you know he didn't talk about the love stuff, but he didn't need to. He defended her leaving, talked about her problems with addiction. He was here all afternoon, checking on you. But as soon as it was time to meet his mom, he got real restless, doing his pacing and jaw clenching."

She takes a sip of her drink. "He was real worried about you, and I can't think of anything that would make that boy leave when he's worried about you. Except for this."

"His mom."

"Yes."

"I need to go back to sleep." I'm too drained, physically and emotionally, to reflect on what

Gran's telling me. She's all worked up, and I can't keep up with her. I give her a kiss on the cheek and crawl back into bed.

It's some time later when I feel a warm body snuggle next to me, and arms wrap around my waist. When he nuzzles my neck, I know it's Jace. I turn to face him and kiss him on the chest. My body melts into his and before I know it, I've fallen back asleep.

When I wake up in the morning, I'm alone in bed and there's no sign that Jace came into my room last night. It may have been a dream.

***

Jace continues to see Annie regularly over the next couple of months. He never invites me. It hurts, but I get it. It was obvious after the first morning I met her that I had a hard time being friendly. And if he's trying to build a relationship with her, my hostility won't be very helpful.

He talks about her occasionally. She got a job waitressing at a French restaurant in town, and she's still staying with an old friend of hers from college. Last week, I saw her sitting in the stands with another woman at Jace's first baseball game of the season. I was running past with my teammates and she didn't notice me.

I skipped our first couple of track meets, telling Coach I wasn't ready to start racing again yet. He's never wanted to push me, but I feel guilty taking advantage of his approach like this. I know I need to get out there again.

I'm in decent shape, as far as I can tell from my workouts with the team. But I'm better at cross than track. Cross country races are longer than track races – and include hills, rocks, and mud. It's just a different style of racing that I've always been more suited for. I can win cross races with ease, but it's always a battle to the finish on the track. And the longer I wait to race, the more the buildup. People are talking about what records I'll break, and who might give me competition. Expectations are building. And I'm trying to ignore all of it.

But today I'm racing for the first time. It's the Rocky Mountain Relays – my favorite track meet. There are no individual races, so I won't be scrutinized as closely. We're trying to qualify for State in the 4 x 800 and the DMR (distance medley relay).

We're in the final heat for the 4 x 800, which means we're seeded amongst the fastest relay teams. Brockton Public won the team state cross country title, but we aren't quite as competitive on the track. In cross, everyone runs the same race, and only a handful of team members can score points. With track, there are tons of different events – sprints, pole vaulting, javelin, long jump. We have strong distance runners, but we only score a small portion of the overall points in a track competition.

Jenny leads the relay, setting us off in third place. Claire slips us back to fourth, and as Zoe comes around the corner, it looks like we're back in third. Not that place really matters too much so early in the season, although it's always nice to win. And a win at the Rocky Mountain Relays is pretty cool.

There's a roar from the crowd as the anchor for the first place team takes the baton, with second place not far behind. I glance at the clock before moving to the inside lane. 7:32 insert time.

The qualifying standard for State is 9:52. That leaves me with 2 minutes and twenty seconds. Seventy seconds for each lap.

I start to jog while reaching back for Zoe to hand off the baton. When I feel the metal hit my palm, I grasp it in my hand. And take off.

Two laps around the track – half a mile – is the shortest distance I ever race. I think of it as a controlled sprint. I'm running hard – *almost* a sprint – but holding back just enough that I don't collapse after one lap.

As I come around the turn to the straightaway after the first lap, I catch the anchor for the second place team. Coach calls out my split – 66 – when I pass through at one lap. My lungs are already burning – the kind of burn I only feel when I'm running an 800.

I'm starting to lap runners from teams that are farther behind, and with all the other runners I can't quite make out how far ahead the girl in first place is. She's from Denver West – the team that's won the state track title for the past two years – and I look for their gold and black jersey.

I pass three more runners who are only on their first lap of the anchor before I see the Denver West uniform. The runner is tiny, but her legs are moving fast. The noise from the crowd picks up when she passes the 600-meter mark and I'm right behind her. I don't even listen to my split, forgetting that the main point of this race is to hit the qualifying standard. When there's a close race like this, I just want to win. It's instinct.

The fun thing about track is you just never know what might be up the competition's sleeve. In cross, you run with someone for a while, and you can get a sense for how tired they are. On the track, someone might look like they've got nothing left, and then they bust out with a final sprint in the last ten meters.

This girl is still going strong as I sidle up to her into the last straightaway. She could have no kick in her at all, or leave me in the dust. All I can do is crank it up a notch and hope it's enough.

My lungs are on fire but I pump my arms and reach deep for another surge of energy. I start to move ahead of her and she responds with a surge of her own. But I don't let up, and she doesn't have enough speed to drop me. I give it one last push and leave her behind as I cross through the finish.

My teammates pat me on the back, ensuring that we hit the qualifying standard. It's nice to get that out of the way early on. But there's nothing that compares to winning a race. It feels good to be back in the game.

Chapter 9

The DMR is the last race of the day, and we qualify for State with time to spare. Unfortunately, I don't pull through for the win, and we take third. After the exhilarating win in the 4 x 800, I got it in my head that maybe I *can* live up to people's expectations. But when I only passed one other team in the DMR, I knew I'd let everyone down.

What happened between the two races today to make it so I did well in one and not so great in the other? That's the million-dollar question. I have no idea why I raced inconsistently and that's what leaves me so upset. Was it the announcer calling me "the Brockton High Phenomenon" that freaked me out? Or was I just tired from racing earlier? Maybe it's because I'm on my period. Who knows?

"Don't be so hard on yourself," Zoe tells me as we get on the bus for the ride home. "You still ran a faster split than I'll ever run."

I swallow. That's the last thing anyone wants to hear when they have a bad race. It makes me feel even worse because I come off as a jerk for being bummed about the race in the first place. But every track runner knows it's not really about how you compare to others. We're disappointed when we don't reach our potential. And all of our potentials are different. I know what mine is. And I didn't reach it today.

Or did I? I don't know what my potential is anymore. Is it what other people are saying about me? That I'm unbeatable? Unstoppable? No. That's not true. I'm just a normal girl who's got some talent. I may already have peaked out.

I sigh and listen to the others talk about their Saturday night plans. Jace texted me that he's going to the Rockies game with his dad and Wes after his baseball game. The three of them hang out a lot together these days. I'm happy that Wes is getting some time with the dad he never had, but I feel a little left out.

Zoe and Charlie are going on a date. Rollie invited people over to his house for pizza but I'm not really in the mood to hang out with my running buddies at the moment. I know they mean well, but I'm tired of deflecting questions about racing and listening to everyone's expectations for me.

My phone rings and I see it's Gran. Maybe she'll be in the mood to lay low and watch a movie with me when she gets back from Royal Feathers – a casino a couple of hours from Brockton.

"Hi, baby girl! How was the meet?"

"It was okay. What's up? You win big?" Gran never wins big because she only plays the slot machines. But I always ask.

"Fifty big ones! And Lulu won a hundred so she's taking me out to dinner. You'll be okay scrounging for dinner, right? We had a few too many cocktails so we're going to spend the night."

"Yeah, sure. No problem, Gran."

Zoe nudges me in the ribs when I hang up the phone. "What did Buns have to say? You look bummed."

"She'll be out tonight, so it's too bad Jace is hanging out with his Dad. That's all."

Zoe wiggles her eyebrows. "Ah... missing an opportunity to have the house to yourself. Yup. Bummer indeed." She smacks her lips. I know her alone-time opportunities with Charlie are limited, and she hasn't spilled too many of the details. She has four younger brothers and sisters, and an over-protective father. As far as I know, Zoe's still in the V club with me.

After a hot bath, I slip on cozy sweatpants and search the cupboards for something to eat for dinner. Even though Dave is by my side as I wait for water to boil for mac and cheese, I can't help but feel lonely.

I've never dwelled on my family situation much before. My parents died before I was old enough to have memories of them. It usually doesn't make me feel sad, because I was too young to experience the sense of loss that normally goes with parents dying. It's been just me and Gran for as long as I can remember. And Wes and Jace, who also had incomplete families. Sure, Wes had both his parents, but we all understood even as kids that they weren't like normal parents.

We spent a lot of time at Wesley's house growing up because he had the pool, the trampoline, and all the other fun stuff that goes with being wealthy. But I only ever met Mr. Jamison a couple of times. He was always away for work. Mrs. Jamison was supposedly around, but we rarely saw her. She had a busy social agenda, from what I remember. She didn't work, but was always off at a luncheon or some event at the country club. Wesley grew up with nannies taking care of him.

Jace had Jim, who can best be described as "the cool dad". Jim took us to do fun stuff, and wasn't much of a disciplinarian. We ate sloppy joes or hot dogs for dinner when he was in charge. There has always been a noticeable lack of maternal influence in the Wilder household.

So it never felt incomplete having Gran as my only parent. Between Wes, Jace and Jim, it was like having a complete family. And now that Wes is back in our lives, shouldn't I be feeling that sense of completeness again?

As I mix noodles and cheese together in a pot, my self-pity shifts to anger. If we were supposed to be each other's family, how could they just decide to break apart while leaving me in the dark? I was miserable the year that Jace and Wes started high school. My best friends went off to high school while I was stuck in the eighth grade. I hadn't discovered running yet, and the girls who befriended me – Tina Anderson and Dana Foster – were social climbers who were just using me to get to Wes and Jace. But most of all, I'd lost one of my closest friends and I had no idea what had broken apart what I had once thought of as my family.

Why didn't Wes fight to stay *my* friend at least, even if he and Jace weren't? Why didn't Jace explain to me what was going on instead of blocking me out? His popularity at Brockton Public meant he had less and less time to hang out with me. He hadn't written me off like Wes had, but lonely Saturday nights became a regular occurrence. The boys no longer came over in their pajamas for movie night. And to top it off, Jim and Gran knew what was going on but neither of them filled me in.

Sighing, I take a bite of mac and cheese and flick a few noodles on the floor for Dave.

The quiet apartment on a Saturday night reminds me of all those times in the eighth grade, when I felt rejected and didn't know why. Freshman year, I discovered running and made new friends with my teammates, and the pain of losing our imperfect happy family gradually lessened.

But the wound got ripped back open from time to time. I remember working at the Tavern one summer night after freshman year. Jace was at a table with a bunch of guys on the football team, and I was bussing tables. When Wesley walked in with his parents, my eyes darted to Jace, who was glaring at the Jamison family in anger. Wes passed me on his way to the table but didn't acknowledge me. It broke my heart all over again. Jace never stopped glaring their way, and eventually he stormed out of the restaurant without saying goodbye. By that point, I'd stopped asking questions.

Now, a fresh wound had been inflicted. That Jace and Wes were brothers explained some of the reasoning for the hurt I went through years ago, but it also makes me feel pushed aside all over again.

A knock on the door startles me from my thoughts. Ryan Harding is the last person I expect to see when I open it. Freshly showered, and wearing dark-wash jeans and a UC hoodie. With his dimpled smile, it's no wonder I fell for him when he moved to Brockton at the beginning of the school year. Despite years of feelings developed for Jace, Ryan managed to find a special place in my heart.

"Hi, Pepper."

"Hi." Heat rises to my cheeks when I remember that I haven't really spoken with him since he saw me collapse on the trail a couple of months ago. Sure, I see him at practice and at school on the time. But it's hard to know how to act around an ex-boyfriend, especially one I still care about so much.

"I was wondering if we could maybe talk?" he asks, almost shyly.

"Sure." I open the door wider. "Want some mac and cheese?" I offer, before taking another bite from the bowl still in my hands.

"I'm good." Ryan pats Dave before settling on a kitchen stool. It's been months since he's been at my apartment, and it's weird having him here now that we're both dating other people.

"So, great races today in the relays," I compliment him, but it just comes out sounding awkward.

"Thanks, you too." Okay, now it's even more awkward. Because I didn't really race well and we both know it. Unless maybe he's referring to my first race.

"Want anything to drink?" I offer. "I think there are some beers in the fridge." I assume he'll decline, but he doesn't. Since apparently he's staying for more than a quick minute, I open a beer for myself as well. Maybe if we're both having a drink this won't be so brutally uncomfortable.

"So, how have you been feeling?" Ryan asks with his eyes lowered to his beer bottle.

"You mean, after the crazy blizzard run?"

He glances up and nods with a small smile.

"I was fine after a good night's sleep and a couple days off from running. But I'm guessing you aren't talking about my physical well-being?" I ask with raised eyebrows.

He frowns in concern. "No, I am." He swallows and shifts in his seat. "I mean, I guess I could tell you didn't get sick or anything and you ran well at practice and stuff." He shrugs sheepishly. "So yeah, maybe I'm more concerned with why you were out there running like that in the first place?" He hasn't exactly asked a question but the tone of his voice tells me he's trying to get answers.

I slide onto the stool next to him and take a sip of my beer, trying to decide what to tell him. He isn't here for gossip, or to get in the middle of me and Jace. Ryan's never had anything but good intentions, but he won't be getting the truth out of me.

"It's complicated, Ryan." There's not much to say without implying that it has something to do with me and Jace, which is inappropriate given Ryan is my ex-boyfriend. Besides, it's bigger than just a boyfriend problem.

Ryan turns to face me. "I'm not trying to be nosy. I'm just concerned, Pepper. That really freaked me out. You were white as a ghost and falling over when I saw you out there. And I can tell your head's not into it with track. I've watched you at practice," he pauses, blushing at how the statement sounds a little stalker-ish. "You're running well, but you just seem bummed out sometimes. If it's about running, you can talk to me."

Well, there's that too. But I don't want to talk about it. Because I don't know what *it* is.

Ryan puts his hand on the back of my chair. "Look, Pepper. I know things are different between us but that doesn't mean I'm not here for you if you need someone to talk to. About anything. Not just running."

"Thanks, Ryan. I'll remember that." But I don't make him the same offer. It's not that I wouldn't be there for him too, but this conversation is already a bit too intimate given the circumstances. "Now, I assume you were on your way to do something more exciting than sitting here with me and Dave on Saturday night."

Ryan laughs. "Not really. I've gotten a couple texts about stuff going on, but there's nothing big happening. I think people are taking it easy after the parties at Remy's and Wesley's last weekend." He hesitates a moment before adding, "Plus, Wesley and Jace are at the Rockies game tonight." He doesn't need to explain the significance of that fact. If those two aren't going to be around, people are less motivated to party.

The front door opens again and Dave scrambles around the kitchen counter to greet Jace and Wes. Speak of the devils.

They call out hello and kick off their shoes before glancing up to see Ryan sitting next to me. Technically, Ryan and Jace are friends, but it's only because they run in the same group with Remy, Ben and Connor.

Jace's smile flattens. "I'm not going to lie, man. It's sort of fucked up that you're hanging out with my girlfriend. Alone." So he's going to blame this on Ryan instead of me. Fair enough. Ryan's the one who came over unannounced, after all.

Ryan jumps up from his stool to confront Wes and Jace. Their stances are intimidating, and I'm impressed that Ryan doesn't stutter in his response. "Sorry if it looks sketchy, Jace. I was just talking to Pepper about running stuff but was on my way to meet up with some guys on the track team." Ryan turns to me and asks, "I take it you're not going to Rollie's, then?" I have a feeling Ryan had no intention of going to Rollie's before this moment, but in an effort to ease the tension, I play along like the track party was the reason Ryan came by.

"Nope. I need a break from running talk."

"You sure, Pep?" Jace asks in a hard voice. "Go if you want to." Okaaay, so he *is* taking this out on me too.

I roll my eyes at his jealous antics, trying to make it seem like this is no big deal. It isn't, right?

"You guys want a beer?" I ask Wes and Jace as I make my way to the fridge, just for something to do. When I pass Jace, I stand on my tiptoes and kiss him on the cheek, hoping it will loosen that clenched jaw.

Wes looks equally menacing, and once again I'm struck by the resemblance between them. There's too much testosterone for our tiny kitchen. It's a relief when Ryan leaves a moment later, his beer still sitting mostly full on the counter.

I hand two bottles to Wes and Jace and sit back down on the counter.

"Did you guys eat dinner? I'm probably going to finish off the mac and cheese but I can make another box."

Jace ignores my attempt to brush off what just happened. He puts his hands on the counter with his arms on either side of me, caging me in. Out of the corner of my eye I watch Wes lean against the wall, watching us.

"Did you invite him over because you thought I'd be out all night at the game?" he asks softly.

I narrow my eyes. "Don't be an asshole, Jace."

"What do you expect me to think? It felt like shit every time I saw you with him when you two were together. Now you're finally my girlfriend and I still have to see you looking all cozy with him?"

"We weren't 'all cozy', Jace. I hardly ever talk to Ryan anymore. Don't make it into something it's not."

Jace shakes his head and pushes away from the counter. He takes a long sip of beer as he walks away from me, down the hall. Our apartment isn't big enough for him to pace and he returns a moment later. He shoots me a hard look before turning back around and sitting on the couch in the living room.

My eyes swing to Wes, who gives me a look that says, *Well, what did you expect?*

I shrug. Jace doesn't exactly have true ex-girlfriends because he's never been monogamous, but if I swung by unexpectedly and saw, say, Madeline Brescoll, sitting next to him in his kitchen, I'd feel pretty shitty about it. But then again, Madeline's a witch with no potential for platonic relationships and Ryan's a good guy and my teammate.

Still.

Jace's reaction is fair, and I should be understanding.

I settle in next to him on the couch and he hits the channels on the remote, ignoring me. When I snuggle up next to him, he's forced to glance my way. I wrap my arms around his waist.

"I'm sorry. There's absolutely nothing funny going on with me and Ryan, okay? Please don't be mad."

We listen to Wes clambering around in the kitchen for a moment, watching each other. Finally, Jace lets out a heavy sigh.

"I really want to be mad for at least a few more minutes but you're making it really hard when you look at me like that."

Ha! I blink innocently, pretending I have no idea what he means even though I know full well that I've got the puppy-dog-eyes look down pat.

"Okay, you can be mad for five more minutes." I check my watch and scoot to the other side of the couch, putting space between us. A second later, Jace hurls himself over to my side and devours me in kisses along my neck and collarbone, running his hands all over my body, squeezing my hips, my bum, and my legs as he does. Oh, if this is Jace mad I'll just have to make him angry more often.

But I know he's just easing his worries by making it clear that I'm his. Jace's possessiveness isn't news to me, and if this is what he needs to do to make it all right, I'm not complaining.

Chapter 10

Movie night with Jace and Wes doesn't exactly feel like old times – the dynamics have changed too much – but it helps soothe the anger I'd felt building earlier that evening. The secret they finally shared with me wasn't meant to push me to the side again, but to help rebuild our family. It won't be the same as it was before, but I'm still part of it. We have our own friends now, and Annie has to fit in somehow too. Of course, the biggest change is between Jace and me.

When Jace kisses me goodnight before heading out with Wes, I realize I'm not the only one who might feel left out at times. Wesley doesn't act bothered by the affection between me and Jace, but he's as good at burying his emotions as Jace is. Except for anger. Neither boy is afraid to show that particular emotion. I suppose it was inevitable that anger was the predominant sentiment between them for so long.

When Dave and I show up for breakfast at the Wilders' the next morning, I don't see anyone in the kitchen but the smell of bacon and coffee tells me I'm in the right place. There are voices coming from the back porch and I see that Jace, Annie and Jim are taking advantage of the unseasonably warm day.

"If you both partied so hard in college, how did Annie end up an addict, and Dad didn't?" I hear Jace ask.

The question makes me pause at the kitchen counter.

No one responds at first, and I imagine Annie and Jim glancing at each other.

"I don't know if I have a good answer to that," Annie says. "I'm still trying to figure it out."

They haven't heard me come in yet, and I feel like I should announce my presence. But I don't want to interrupt the conversation. It's an important one, and it might not happen again. It's not every day Jace Wilder asks probing questions that are guaranteed to have an emotional response.

I busy myself pouring orange juice and loading my plate with pancakes and bacon while listening through the open window.

Jace must be giving her one of his looks that says she better try harder than that because after a moment, Annie speaks again.

"I started doing drugs probably for the same reason most people do. They make you feel good. They're fun. I wish I could blame it on something like a rough childhood or a tragic event, but I think what it really comes down to is selfishness."

My heart stops for a beat. If she's admitting to being selfish, it makes it a lot harder to hate her. And it's a lot easier to hate her than to forgive her. I don't *want* to forgive her.

"When Jim became a dad, the partying was just over. He knew being a dad was more important. I guess I just wanted to keep having fun, and maybe it was guilt that turned it into something more than harmless partying. I don't know. But before I knew it, I couldn't go a day without getting high on something."

"And so you just left?" Jace asks. His voice isn't accusing or angry, but genuinely curious, like he really just wants to understand his mother.

"I had a new boyfriend by then, and he was moving to the east coast. I probably thought it was a way to escape the guilt weighing on me from being such a lousy mom. If I wasn't around to be reminded of how I was failing as a mother, and to know how much I was missing out on, then it would be easier. Or so I thought at the time. Of course, I convinced myself you'd be better off without me. Which still might be true."

"Mom," Jace tries to interrupt. It's the first time I've heard him call her that. And I don't like it.

"No, Jace, it's true. I probably would have just made life harder for you and Jim. Anyway, getting away didn't make anything better. That's when the drugs got really out of control. Eventually I realized I had a real problem and tried to get better, but it's been up and down ever since."

"Maybe now that you're back here you can stay sober. I'll help you," Jace tells her. He sounds confident and hopeful. It breaks my heart a little, because I don't believe Annie will ever be the mom Jace is looking for.

If I hadn't already filled up my plate, I'd sneak back out the front door. But my banana pancakes are doused in butter and syrup and there's no way I'm letting them go to waste.

"Morning, guys," I say as I slide open the door to the patio.

"Hi, Pepper!" Jim stands up to give me a hug, a little more enthusiastically than usual. I take it he's relieved to have a break from the heavy conversation. "I'm getting a coffee refill, anyone else want one?"

"I'll take some more, Dad," Jace says, handing his mug to Jim.

Jace slides his arm out around my waist as I pass him and I gladly lean into him. He pulls me onto his lap, and I can't suppress the smile that takes over my face. Jace has become increasingly open with his affections toward me, and I don't think it will ever get old. Annie's in my seat again anyway, so I'm happy to share with Jace.

"So, you were talking about addiction?" I make eye contact with Annie and pop a mouthful of pancake in my mouth. I'm really tempted to make a bratty remark about how wanting to feel good is a lame excuse for Annie's problem, and for leaving Jace. Why can't she just do something like go for a run to feel good? But I refrain from being a brat for Jace's sake and instead give her a questioning look as I munch away.

"Yes. We were talking about why the college party scene took me in one direction while it didn't take Jim down the same road."

"Right. Jim finished school and started working harder when he had a kid." I take a sip of orange juice, not bothering to fill in what Annie chose to do, by contrast.

As I swallow, I realize Annie could point out that Jim also managed to get another woman – a married woman, at that – pregnant at the same time. Instead, Annie just nods, accepting that she was a shitty person. "Jim's been a great dad, hasn't he?" she asks, just as he returns with two full coffee mugs.

"Hmmm... I don't know about that," he says with a chuckle. "I don't know what I would have done without your grandma, Pepper. Bunny kept you kids in line."

I raise my eyebrows. "You sure about that?"

He points his fork in our direction. "Well, this one still manages to get into some trouble, but he's turned out okay, I guess." Jim grins, showing off the Wilder charm.

I leave the Wilders' as soon as I finish my pancakes. Annie's presence in their home makes me uneasy. She brings out a side of me that I don't like.

I recognize Wesley's car turning onto Shadow Lane as I walk down the sidewalk with Dave. He pulls up next to me and leans out the window. "Don't tell me I'm too late for pancakes," he says.

"There's still some left, but you might not enjoy the company," I warn.

"Jim's girl is over? I like Sheila," he tells me.

"No. Annie is over there." I walk across the road to his car. "Have you met her yet?"

Wes sighs. "Not yet. I should probably just get it over with, but you look like you could use some company."

He waits for me to run up to the apartment for my books. We head to Muddy's, a café near the UC campus where I sometimes do my homework.

We find a table outside where Dave can join us. Wes gets a muffin and coffee while I sip on lemonade.

"I take it you aren't a fan of Annie, huh?" he asks.

I shrug. "She left Jace. So no, I don't like her," I tell him honestly.

Wes watches me. "Jace seems to have forgiven her," he says, stating the obvious.

"Yeah. I know. I don't get it."

"Me either," he says simply. "I figure it's not my business and it's better to stay out of it. I'm just trying to be his brother, you know? I'll be around if he needs me."

"You're lucky you have an excuse to stay out of it," I tell him. We both know what I'm referring to. "I feel like a bitch that I'm not on board with Jace's loving feelings toward her."

"He gets it. Don't worry about it," Wes says, putting a comforting hand on my arm.

We settle in with our homework for a couple of hours, until Wes realizes he's getting a sunburn. "I should probably head to the gym anyway before I get too lazy," he says with a stretch.

"Yeah, and I should give Dave the Sunday run he looks forward to all week."

I'm packing up my books while Wes heads back inside to use the restroom, when I hear a familiar voice.

"You really can't just stick to one guy, can you?" Emma asks. "Madeline won't be pleased to hear that you're opening your legs for Lincoln Academy guys now too."

I glance up at Madeline Brescoll's sidekicks.

"She's got a thing for Brockton's golden boys. First Ryan, then Jace. Now she's already moved on to Wesley," Serena says while giving me a disgusted look.

"Lucky you. You'll get passed around to all three of them before they graduate," Emma says condescendingly.

"So, doing homework at a café with a friend means sleeping with him too? That's a stretch, don't you think?" I ask in a bored tone. Without Madeline's presence, their snide remarks are easier to shake off. Besides, they really are grasping at straws.

Emma opens her mouth to respond, but shuts it when Wesley joins us. She smiles at him. "Hi, Wes. We missed you at Pierce's place last night."

"I was at Pepper's place," Wes tells her. "With Jace," he adds in an annoyed tone, after Serena and Emma share a knowing look.

When we get to his car, Wes asks me, "Do I need to handle those girls? Are they giving you a hard time?"

"Ugh! You sound like Jace!" I say in exasperation.

Wes chuckles. "Well, we *are* brothers."

"I can handle a couple of bitchy girls, okay? Why are you friends with them, anyway?" I ask.

Wes rolls down his window with a smirk. "They're hot, I guess."

"You're such a guy."

"Can't argue with that."

It's been a long time since Wes and I hung out, just the two of us. It's nice to know that he's the same goofy, easy-going boy I remember. But he's also kind of an asshole about girls, which is new to me.

Maybe he just needs to meet someone special. After all, his half-brother shared the same fault before we got together.

Jace shows up at our apartment later that night right when I'm getting ready for bed.

He sits on my bed with Dave while I brush my hair.

"So, what'd you think about Annie's explanation for leaving?" I ask. We make eye contact in the mirror. I know I'm pushing him somewhere he probably doesn't want to go, but I really need to understand where he's at with his mom.

"So you heard her talking about it?" he asks.

"Yeah. I heard her say she became an addict because doing drugs makes her feel good. And she left because she had a new boyfriend who was moving east."

Jace holds my gaze. "Yeah, well, at least she was honest. And you know what?" he asks, his voice defensive. "I get it. I get her."

I spin around slowly. It's not what I want to hear, but at least he's opening up.

"You know, getting high does feel good. No one can deny that. I never really did much because of sports, but it's easy to see how you could start doing it too much. I know plenty of guys who do. And you saw me last fall."

Jace had been dealing drugs with Wesley, but hadn't been doing drugs himself. That changed when I started dating Ryan. Who knows how far it would have gone if Wes and I hadn't intervened.

"How can I judge her when I've been far from perfect myself?" Jace places his hands on my hips and I step between his open knees.

I remember that Wes said he was just trying to be a good brother. I try to just be a good girlfriend by listening to Jace, and holding back my opinion. He needs to figure it out on his own, and the last thing I want is for him to close me out and feel like he can't talk to me. So I keep my mouth shut and brush his hair back from his forehead.

He leans his head forward, resting it on my tummy, and I continue stroking his head, sensing he just needs comfort right now.

Gran bursts in, breaking the quiet moment.

"All right, kiddos, no shenanigans. At least not when I'm home! Time for bed," she says, shaking her finger at us, and it's hard not to giggle given that she's wearing an Elmo pajama set. I wonder if they sell those in adult sizes or if she managed to fit into a kid size. "In your own beds," she clarifies before shutting the door and marching off, her piglet slippers oinking with each step.

Jace and I smile at each other and he kisses me on the nose before following Gran's orders.

Chapter 11

I find myself alone again the following Saturday night, but this time I don't wallow in self-pity or simmer in anger. Jim's got season tickets so the boys are at another Rockies game with him. We didn't have a meet today, just a hard workout. I don't have any trouble running fast at practice, so hopefully I'll be able to follow through with racing at the next meet.

After showering and changing into yoga pants and a comfy sweater, I order some Chinese food for dinner. Instead of waiting for delivery, I take the opportunity to give Dave some exercise and we take the fifteen-minute walk to campus. One good thing about living near UC is that there are lots of takeout options close by. It never compares to Gran's cooking, but it's nice to shake it up once in a while.

Since it's Saturday night, the college kids are out in full force. They always seem to travel in groups. And even on brisk spring nights like tonight, the girls are scantily dressed. What's up with that? For the first time, I find myself actually curious about college life. I've never put much thought into what goes on just down the street from my apartment. But Jace will be a student here soon. Naturally, my interest is piqued. What will he be up to in just a few short months?

I pull up the hood of my sweater after hooking Dave to a tree outside the Chinese joint. While the masses around me are going out to do who knows what, I plan to take my dinner home and get ahead on homework.

The door swings out, and Kayla Chambers nearly knocks me over. Her hands are full with bags of food.

"Oh, hey Pepper! Sorry about that."

I hold the door open. "No worries."

"You grabbing dinner?" She blows long blonde strands out of her face. As the leader of the most popular senior girls at Brockton Public, she pulls off the Barbie look well.

"Yeah, just laying low with my dog tonight." I nod toward Dave, who's licking his chops at the smell emanating from the store.

"Oh, really? Why don't you come hang out with us? It's just me, Andrea and Lisa relaxing."

I've gotten to know the three girls a little more over the past couple of months. Kayla and Andrea are pretty friendly, but Lisa remains stand-offish.

"Oh, that's okay. Thanks, though." Who wants to accept a pity invite?

"You should come! Come on, it'll be fun. I'm parked right up the street and on my way. I can give you and Dave a ride."

"You know my dog's name?"

She shrugs. "Yeah, you've talked about him before. And Jace talks about him a lot, too."

"Okay, why not? Let me just grab my food."

***

We pull up to a house in the same neighborhood where Omar lives. It's a modest two story, with a two-car garage.

"The Hills are visiting Andrea's sister at college in Kansas, so we've got the place to ourselves," Kayla explains as we head inside. "Oh, and I'm going to drink tonight, so I won't be able to give you a ride home. But you can crash here with us if you want."

"Okay, we'll see. Dave can come in, right?" I cringe, realizing I should have cleared that beforehand.

"Yeah. He'll get along great with Murphy, the Hills' dog."

I follow Kayla through the front door, with Dave beside me.

"Hey girls!" Kayla calls out. "I texted ahead of time so they know you're coming," she tells me.

We find Andrea and Lisa on a couch in the living room drinking pink wine. There's a box of Franzia on the coffee table.

"Hi, Pepper!" Andrea smiles and waves. "Got you girls some wine glasses, so fill 'em up."

Lisa says hello, slightly less enthusiastically, before returning to typing something on her cell phone.

"The guys are watching the game at Connor's place and we didn't feel like it, so we're just having a girl's night," Andrea explains as she starts opening the Chinese food boxes. "Oh, I should put the dogs out or Murphy will totally try to eat our dinner." She hops up to let the dogs outside.

Kayla hands me a glass of pink wine and I settle into an armchair with my sesame chicken.

Two glasses of wine later, I'm starting to feel a little more comfortable. The girls have been chatting away about all kinds of things that don't interest me – like what sorority they'll join in college – but at least it's distracting me from all the things I don't want to think about.

"So, Pepper…" Kayla turns to me. "Has Madeline given you any shit since the party at Remy's a couple months ago?"

My eyebrows shoot up. How does she know about that? "Not really."

I scoot forward in my chair to refill my wine glass. My head is starting to spin a little, but I'm feeling relaxed and I like it.

"Hmmm," Kayla reflects. "She may not have said anything to you directly, but she's trying to stir up trouble."

My eyes flick to hers. "She is?"

Kayla nods with a sympathetic smile. "Come on. Madeline doesn't declare war on you like she did and then walk away. I know you're a little naïve, Pepper, but you didn't think she'd just disappear, did you?"

I shrug. "Well, no. I mean, I've seen her around."

I don't think Kayla intended to insult me, because there's no snideness in her tone. And anyway, I'd rather be the one oblivious to social drama than the one instigating it. But what about being the victim? Is that what she's telling me?

"Where's Jace tonight?" Lisa asks. "He's not at Connor's with the other guys."

That comment, on the other hand, was intended to rile my feathers. I let her know it didn't by gazing back at her impassively.

Andrea glares at Lisa, who shrinks back on the couch. "He's at the game with Wesley, Lisa," she says sharply. "Although Lisa does have a point. No need to get paranoid, but Madeline has definitely been trying to move in on your man, and it's best you know about it."

I gulp down another sip of wine. Shit. How did I not know this?

"Look, Pepper. We like you," Kayla says. My eyes slide to Lisa. Who is *we* exactly?

Kayla answers my unasked question "Well, Lis here needs to get over that you used to date her boyfriend, but she's got your back."

Lisa nods in agreement, though her icy attitude tells me she's only on board to avoid conflict with her best friends.

"Anyway, we never liked Madeline hanging around Jace, acting like they had something special." She must recognize the hurt look on my face because she adds, "It *wasn't* anything special. We all got that he had a thing for you. Believe me. Sure, didn't stop us from..."

Andrea coughs and glares at Kayla. Right, they've all hooked up with him. At least, according to rumors.

"Yeah, well, you know. So the point is, we don't like Madeline and her girls. They're bitches. We put up with them because Jace seems to like hanging with Wesley these days, and that means Lincoln people are going to be around at parties, but I do *not* want those girls moving in on our territory."

I frown. What exactly does she mean by territory? Their popularity and power at Brockton Public? Or maybe she means the guys? Both, I guess.

"Serena is always all over Connor. It drives me nuts," Andrea says. "I mean, we're going to different colleges next year, and we finally have something good together. I won't let her mess with my last few months with him."

"Do you know why Wes and Jace are so close now, anyway?" Lisa asks me.

I look down at my wine glass and swirl around the pink liquid. These girls surely knew about the drug dealing, and they also probably know that's not happening anymore. It's a fair question, but I'm not going to be the one to give the full answer.

"They used to be really close. I guess they just reconnected." It's not exactly a lie.

All three girls watch me, and I know they sense I'm not telling the full truth.

"What did you mean that Madeline is trying to move in on Jace?" I ask Kayla.

She shrugs and leans back in her chair. "At first, she was moving in on Wesley. She probably thought it would make Jace jealous or something, since Wesley and Jace used to have some sort of rivalry. But Jace didn't give a shit."

I remember her little display at the ping pong tournament. I also remember Jace looking angry. Had he been jealous? Or was he mad because he recognized she was using Wes to get his attention? Do brothers get protective of each other over stuff like that?

Kayla continues, "Now she's just going right for Jace. I've seen her in seduction mode a few times around him."

My blood boils. I know exactly what Kayla is talking about by "seduction mode". I have seen Madeline work her magic, and it's quite effective. Guys lose their cool big time when she turns on the charm.

Andrea shakes her head and laughs. "Yeah, but Jace doesn't give her the time of day. It's so satisfying to witness."

"Did you see her after our tennis match the other day when Jace was leaving practice?" Lisa says with a giggle.

Kayla rolls her eyes. "Yeah, he made a fool of her. But I don't know how long that will last. I've never seen a guy turn her down."

The other girls look at each other and fidget. It's clear from their uneasy expressions that Madeline has messed with the guys they are currently seeing.

"We just need to watch her. She'll change tactics at some point." I can see why Kayla is the leader of the group. She's thinking ahead. She knows how this scheming game works because she's probably played at it herself. How else do you become the most powerful girl at Brockton Public? Not by sitting back and going with the flow, that's for sure. Because that's just what I've been doing, and apparently it's unwise of me.

Chapter 12

"Boys are here!" Andrea announces some time later that night. We've been playing cards and I have no idea how much time has passed.

Remy, Connor and Ryan enter the living room and laugh at the mess we've left on the coffee table. Remy lifts the box of Franzia. "Damn, girls, you finish this all tonight?"

We giggle in response, providing him with his answer.

"Where's Ben?" I ask. Remy frowns at me. Maybe that was a stupid question. "It's just, usually he's with you guys," I say quietly.

"Oh, he went to hook up with some girl," Remy tells me.

I nod, realizing these guys each have a girl here, and I'm the odd one out. Awkward.

"When did the game end?" I wonder.

"About an hour ago," Connor tells me.

Oh. Jace should be back soon. Unless they went somewhere. But I don't have my phone on me so I have no idea if he wanted to meet up.

"Did you want to check in with Jace?" Remy asks, as though reading my mind.

"Yeah. Can I use your phone?" I stand up, and waver for a second before catching my balance. Whoa. I definitely need to stop drinking.

Remy walks over to me and takes my arm. "Easy there. You okay?"

"Yeah, yeah. I'm good."

He hands me his phone and I head into the hallway to call Jace. As I scroll through Remy's contacts I overhear him talking to Kayla. "How much did she drink? Jace might not be down with this."

"She's a big girl, Remy. She's been coming out and drinking since they got together. It's no big deal."

"Yeah, but Jace is always with her when she's been out before. And I've never really seen her drunk."

Well, maybe it's about time I do get drunk. My body feels nice and loose, like a noodle. And I really want to see Jace.

"What's up?" Jace answers.

I frown. That's not usually how he answers when I call. Oh, right. He thinks it's Remy calling.

"Hey, it's Pepper," I tell him.

Jace's tone softens immediately and it makes me smile. "Oh, Pep," he sounds relieved. "I was wondering where you were. I just got to your place and no one's home. I was trying to reach you earlier. Where you at?"

"I'm at Andrea Hill's house. Do you know where she lives? You should come over. Everyone else has a boyfriend here and I want you to come."

Jace doesn't say anything for a beat. "Have you been drinking?"

"You can tell?"

"Yeah, your voice is girlier or something when you drink. It's cute."

"Oh."

"I'm on my way," he tells me.

When I hand Remy his phone, he gives me a glass of water. "You should drink this. You'll feel better in the morning."

I shrug and take the glass from him before returning to my spot on the floor with Dave. There's space for me on the couch, but it feels good to lie down.

This is strange. Hanging out with all of Jace's friends without Jace. But kind of cool too. And I haven't thought about running all night.

I can tell when Jace arrives before he says anything. It's like the energy in the room just shifts in his direction.

The guys get up to greet him and Andrea grabs him a beer from the fridge. He takes a sip but puts it down and heads over to me.

His eyebrows are raised when he looks down at me. "Whatchya doin' down there, Pep?" The corners of his mouth turn up in amusement.

"Dave wanted to hang out with me. You wanna join us?"

Jace shakes his head and laughs. "Sure, Pep."

He bends down and lies next to me, putting his arm under my head and tugging me to him.

We lie there together for a few minutes, catching up on each other's day.

"Hey! I forgot. Gran's at some old ladies' retreat in the mountains. You can sleep over."

"Old ladies' retreat?" he asks in amusement.

I roll my eyes. "I honestly have no idea what it is. That's just what she calls it. Maybe they all sit around knitting."

"It's probably much less innocent than that if Buns is there. And Lulu. Those two together are double trouble."

His assessment sends me into a fit of giggles and Jace shakes his head, smiling at me. A moment later, Jace scoops me up and shifts me to his back for a piggyback ride.

"All right, we're outta here," he announces as he marches out the door. I cling to his back and check to make sure Dave is following us.

We wave goodbye and Jace buckles me in. I start to get sleepy on the drive home, and Jace carries me up to the apartment. He helps me into my pajamas, and snuggles in beside me.

"You never told me that Madeline has been trying to get in your pants," I tell him on a yawn.

"No. Why would you want to know that? I shut her down, Pep. So it's not important."

"Okay. Those girls are all worked up, telling me about some war with her." I snuggle in closer, suddenly not caring about the drama. "Let's just stay out of it."

"You always have, Pep. No need to change that now."

"Yeah, you're right." Or is he? Now that I'm his girlfriend, is it still possible to stay out of it?

Jace strokes my back. "Are you ever going to want to spend some time with my mom? I know you don't like her, but she's becoming a part of my life, and I'd like you to get to know her a little."

Huh? He wants me to get to know her? I thought he was hiding me from her. He's right though. I don't really want to spend time with her. But I will for him.

"Sure, Jace. But only if we can make out a little before I fall asleep."

Jace pulls me on top of him with a groan and grants my request.

***

I wake up with a dry mouth and my face smooshed against Jace's chest. I creep out of his arms and chug two glasses of water before brushing my teeth and climbing back in bed.

"How you feelin'?" Jace asks as he nuzzles my neck.

"Hungry," I tell him. "I'm craving bacon."

Jace laughs. "How are you not hung over? You could barely walk last night."

"How do you know? You carried me everywhere."

He squeezes my hips where I'm ticklish and I slap his hands away. "I carried you *because* you couldn't walk," he explains.

"Oh."

"You're a sweet drunk though." He kisses my collarbone and shoulder.

"I thought you'd be mad. Give me a lecture or something."

"That'd be a little hypocritical of me, don't you think?" He sits up on his elbow and props his head in his hand. "But we do have some stuff to talk about. So I'm gonna run home and get changed, and then I'm taking you to Hal's."

After waiting outside for a table to open up, we slide into a booth at Hal's Diner and order the $4.99 special. The Wilders are out of pancake ingredients so we have to forgo our usual Sunday morning breakfast.

"Pep, I know something's up with you and running. You never talk about racing anymore. You don't seem excited about it. What's up?"

I sigh. Here we go. Time to hash this out.

"It's the pressure. The expectations. Everyone expects me to be the best now. Before, people had confidence in me. And that felt good. But now, it's different. It's like if I don't do well, they'll be disappointed."

Jace tilts his head to the side. "What do you mean by 'they'? Who, exactly?"

I shrug. "Everyone, I guess."

"Not me. Not Gran. We just want you to have fun out there. We're always proud of you when you have a great race, but only because we know you love it."

I think about that. Yeah, I guess that's true. "But what about my teammates, and just, you know, all the people at Brockton Public and in Brockton who have been following my running?"

"You really think your teammates would be disappointed in you? And who cares about fans you don't even know?"

Maybe he's right. But still, the pressure weighs on me. "Do you ever feel it with football? The expectations? Doesn't it get to you?"

"Yeah, of course." He sounds surprised that I asked. "You can't tell?"

"Seriously? You act so chill about it, and you've never said anything."

"I could tell you were feeling it because I get that way too. Maybe it motivates some people, knowing everyone's watching and critiquing, but it messes with me. I just want to play well because I love it. It's cool when we have a crowd and people are really into it, but the hype about how I'm playing is a distraction. So I just try to block it out, you know?"

"Kinda. I was on two relays at the Rocky Mountain Relays last weekend. The first one, once I got moving, I blocked it out and had a great race. The second one, I don't know what happened. I just didn't have it. I didn't feel it."

Jace traces his finger along my thigh. It's distracting me but he hardly seems to notice he's doing it.

"That happens to any athlete, Pep. Just because more people are paying attention doesn't mean you're not gonna have races that don't go well."

"Yeah, I guess every race can't be a great one. I mean, I've had some pretty disastrous ones over the years. But I never felt scared it would happen before the race began. Usually, I assume it'll go well but now, I assume it won't. Or at least it won't go as well as other people think it should."

I put my hand down to join his on my leg, stilling his movements. He uses his other hand to tuck a loose strand of hair behind my ear.

"You just gotta accept that you're gonna have some bad races and people might say some mean stuff that isn't true. But it's worth it, because you love racing."

"When did you turn into such a smarty-pants?" I tease.

"It's sports. I can talk sports," Jace says with a grin. That's true, but he's talking about emotions too, and it's good to see him opening up.

We finish our meal and Jace pays the bill. He takes my hand again as we head out the door and walk down the sidewalk toward his Jeep. I've noticed he likes to make sure we're touching somehow whenever we're together.

"So, the other thing I wanted to talk to you about..." Jace pauses and clears his throat. I glance up at him, curious about the nervousness in his voice. There's a wrinkle in his forehead and I squeeze his hand, hoping he'll relax.

"My mom. She's asked me to invite you to dinner a couple times now." Jace leans me against the passenger door when we reach the car and puts his hands on my hips. "You haven't said anything, but I can tell how you feel about her, and about me spending time with her."

I swallow. Is it fair for me to hold a grudge against her when it's Jace that she hurt?

"Just, can you give her a chance? This is important to me," he says softly.

I brush a lock of hair out of his eyes. "Of course." How can I refuse a request like that from my boyfriend? "It's just hard for me to understand how you can forgive her and trust her so easily after all this time. But, if you have, and you want a relationship with her, I'll do my best to get on board."

He kisses my jaw. "I guess I feel like I understand when people make mistakes and do stupid things. She regrets it, and it just took her a while to get well enough to come back. I've never been an addict, but I get how all-consuming the stuff is. Don't let me turn to that shit again, okay?"

"I won't."

"Come on, let's get some homework done and then we'll meet my mom for dinner."

To my surprise, Jace brings all his books over and studies diligently beside me for several hours. I know he has to get homework done at some point, but I rarely witness it.

He talks me into going to the UC gym later in the afternoon and I do some light lifting while watching girls ogle Jace. And these are college girls. Sheesh.

I'm going through the motions on the leg machines, but I still don't feel like I'm pushing myself with any specific goal in mind. I understand what Jace was saying, but I'm still afraid. I can't just block out the hype around my running success. And it seems like no matter what, I'll never live up to others' expectations. Once you've won a national title, there's nowhere to go but down.

On the drive to Annie's house, I try to psych myself up and get into the same mindset as Jace. She was young when she had him. She had an addiction. She's trying to make up for it now. She's a good person. Who won't hurt Jace. Ugh. I just can't bring myself to believe it.

Annie's roommate, Helen, answers the door, and we follow her into the living room. "Annie will be home any minute. Her shift at the restaurant went later than expected. What can I get you kids to drink?"

We settle in on the couch and Helen brings us lemonade. They live in a two-story condo that's clean and decorated in a modern, minimalist style.

"Pepper, I hear you're quite the runner! I actually heard about you before Annie moved in and Jace started coming around. He's very proud of you."

"Thanks."

"You two sure are the Brockton superstars! And with Jace going to UC next year, he'll probably be starting quarterback as a freshman. People are going to just love having a local boy bring the team back."

Jace and I exchange glances. Yup, those are the expectations laid out for him. I never thought about how he deals with even worse pressure to perform well than I do. Football's way more popular than running, after all.

Annie shows up a few minutes later with bags of food.

"Sorry I'm late! One of the girls on the dinner shift had something come up with her kids and needed me to cover for her for a couple hours after I finished the lunch shift."

I get the feeling she's the kind of person who is always late and always with an excuse.

Jace stands up to meet her in the kitchen and help with the bags.

"I'm glad you could make it, Pepper! Do you like Thai food? I got a mix of different things so hopefully there's something here you like. You aren't on any special diet for running, are you?"

I shake my head. "No, I love Thai food. Sounds great."

Why does this woman rub me the wrong way? *Get over it, Pepper!* I yell at myself. Jace has. You can too.

While we put the food out, Annie asks Jace about his baseball game yesterday. I'm surprised when he tells her that he went to the Rockies game with Wesley and Jim. Isn't Wesley Jamison a sore subject?

But Annie's response has me second-guessing all my assumptions. "Oh, that's wonderful, Jace. It's great to hear the three of you are spending time together."

Huh? Okay, so she's not bitter that Jim got another girl pregnant while she was pregnant with Jace. Weird. Jace better not think *I'd* be okay with that.

When we sit down to eat, Annie turns her attention to me. Unsurprisingly, she asks me questions about running.

She looks better than when I saw her a couple of months ago. There aren't dark circles under her eyes, and she's gained a little weight. Her teeth aren't all that great, and her skin is more wrinkled than it should be at her age. But there's no doubt she was a beauty back in the day. And she still has Jace's striking eyes (they will always be Jace's in my mind, even if he got them from her) and dark, wavy hair. If it wasn't for years of addiction, she'd be stunning.

We sit around talking for a couple of hours before saying goodbye. When I leave, it's not so much anger I feel toward the woman, but pity. She's all nerves. And insecure. It's strange to meet a 40-year-old woman who doesn't seem comfortable in her own skin. Maybe she'll settle down once she gets used to sobriety.

But what surprises me the most is that she doesn't seem to have an ounce of backbone. Sure, she's trying to make up for abandoning her son and it's appropriate for her to act apologetic, but I get the impression she never stands up for herself. And that just jars me because Jace isn't like that one bit.

As we drive home it occurs to me that maybe Jace's protective nature is at play here. He's always been like that toward me, even though I think I can handle myself just fine. Is Jace trying to save his mother? I sure hope not, because that's not a burden he should have to carry.

Chapter 13

Coach Tom pulls me over to talk after practice later that week. I knew I couldn't avoid this conversation much longer.

"Have you thought about your goals for the season?" he asks. We're sitting in the bleachers by the softball field, and I watch my teammates stretch on the other side of the field.

"Not really," I admit. "What do you think my goals should be?"

He shakes his head. "You know that's not how I like to do this, Pepper. First, you tell me what you're thinking, and I'll let you know if I think those goals are reasonable. Then we talk about a plan for the season."

I sigh. "I know. I just don't want to have any goals this season. Is that an option?"

"Why don't you want to have any goals? You've always been a goal-oriented athlete, Pepper."

"I just want to have fun. I want to enjoy it. Everyone else seems to have expectations for me. Do I really need to put more on myself?"

"Goals aren't expectations, Pepper. You know that."

He's right. Maybe if I can focus on a goal, I can forget about other people's expectations.

"Okay, how about winning the 2-mile at State?"

Coach nods in approval. "That's a great goal. You placed second last year in 10:45. And how about the mile? You've doubled with those two events the past two years."

"Can I just focus on the 2-mile and relays? I'll probably be in two relays this year, right?"

"I can put you in three events max at State. So, if you do the 4 x 800 and the DMR, the 2-mile will be your only individual race."

"That's fine."

"Okay. But why don't we put you in the mile at Districts then? You can shoot for first at that meet."

"Sure. Whatever."

"What about times? We can't control who your competition is, but the beauty of track is that we can shoot for some time goals."

"You said I ran 10:45 last year?"

"Yes, that's your PR in the 2-mile. And it's 5:02 in the mile." PR means personal record in running lingo.

"How about 10:40 in the 2-mile and breaking five in the mile?"

"The State meet record is 10:36."

"Fine! I'll try to get that, then."

Why does this feel like a negotiation?

Coach shakes his head. "Look, Pepper, what's going on? You're doing well in practice. You ran some great splits on the relays. I don't understand why you're so reluctant to talk about your racing plan for the season. We normally would have had this conversation weeks ago."

Ignoring his question, I ask the one I really don't want to hear the answer to. "What about Nationals? Should I be thinking about that?"

"Only if you want." Coach goes on to explain that there are two major national meets, and when and where they take place. But I zone out after I hear the words "only if you want." I don't want to train for Nationals. Just the thought of it exhausts me. And if Coach isn't pushing it, then I'm not going for it.

"Judging by the look on your face, I'm guessing you don't want to put Nationals on the racing agenda this season."

"Nope."

"Okay, then let's talk about the plan for the next eight weeks leading to State."

Eight weeks? It seems so short. I guess I've wasted a lot of time already. Coach talks me through the meet schedule, and writes down what events I'll plan to do at each one. I'm only half-listening.

What if I can't even win at State?

I head back to the locker room instead of rejoining the team to stretch. They'll be disappointed I'm not going for Nationals.

The tennis team is leaving when I head into the girls' locker room. Lisa gives me a tight smile while Andrea and Kayla make themselves comfortable on the bench by my locker.

"What are you up to tonight, Pepper?" Kayla asks.

"Uh, homework?" It's Wednesday night. What else would I be doing?

"You should come hang out at Lou's with us," she says.

"Well, my Gran usually expects Jace and me for dinner..." Although she doesn't mind when I change plans on occasion. Usually for something related to running or a class project. But Lou's does have the best pizza in town.

"No problem. We'll invite the guys too," Andrea says happily. She reminds me of Zoe sometimes. Always so... cheerful.

I shrug. "Sure, why not? I'll just take a quick shower here then. Jace can give me a ride when he gets done with practice."

"They might not be done for a bit, so we'll wait on you outside," Kayla says before standing up. Lisa and Andrea follow her out the door and I shake my head, uncertain about being included with their group. They weren't so bad on Saturday night. I had fun, actually. Sighing, I strip down and wrap myself in a towel on my way to the showers.

Dorothy Sandoval stands in front of the only open shower stall wearing a tennis skirt and a sports bra. Her arms are crossed over her chest and the pursed lips tell me she isn't blocking my path by accident.

"What's up, Dorothy?" I ask tentatively. Dorothy runs on the cross country team in the fall, but plays tennis in the spring. She idolizes the Barbies and constantly gossips about them. We're teammates during cross season, but not exactly friends. I don't think any of the girls on the cross team are considered friendship-eligible by Dorothy's standards.

"So, you have new friends now, I see?" she asks bitterly.

I roll my eyes and try to squeeze past her. I've never been a big Dorothy fan, but I don't mind tolerating her. She's been fairly nice to me in the past because of my friendship with Jace. But now that I'm becoming friends with the same girls she's wanted to be friends with for the past four years, all pretense of cordiality has gone out the window. This petty jealousy is not something I want to deal with.

Dorothy moves to the side, forcing me to look her in the eye. "How's tennis going, Dorothy?" Maybe diversion will work.

"Kayla and I are on a doubles team together."

"Oh, that's great."

"But they never invite me to Lou's. Now that you're dating Jace Wilder, you're suddenly good enough to be their friend, is that it?"

"Good enough? You know I don't care about that."

"Maybe you've changed."

"No. I hang out with Jace's friends more now that we're together, that's all. If you want to come to Lou's with us you can." Not that I want to hang out with Dorothy, but maybe inviting her will get her off my back. Who cares if Kayla gets pissed I included someone in their exclusive group?

"I don't need your pity invite, Pepper." She knocks my shoulder as she brushes past me and I have to cover my mouth to contain my laughter.

I really hope that girl gets over her social climbing obsession when she leaves high school. It's just sad.

Thirty minutes later I'm sitting at a large circular booth at Lou's with the Barbies and a pitcher of beer. "So, how come they didn't card you guys?"

"My uncle owns Lou's," Kayla says. "You didn't know that?"

I shake my head and grab a stick of garlic bread. Apparently Kayla didn't get the Italian genes with her blonde hair and blue eyes.

I suppose if I was a Barbie-wannabe like Dorothy that would be good information to know.

"That was her cousin who took our order," Lisa tells me.

"She has some fiiiiine cousins," Andrea says with a giggle.

I smile. The waiter was hot, no question. Dark hair, olive skin. It was probably the similarities to Jace that had me looking him over. Normally I wouldn't look twice at a guy in his twenties.

 "What the hell is Dorothy Sandoval doing here with *them*?" Lisa asks darkly.

We turn our heads to the entrance and watch Dorothy slide into a booth next to Madeline, Serena, and Emma.

My heart rate picks up. This can't be good.

Kayla sends a warning look in their direction. It would probably make most girls squirm, at the very least, but Madeline ignores her. She bats her eyelashes at Kayla's cousin, and he leans over the table to get a better look at her cleavage.

I had no intention of drinking beer tonight, but it suddenly looks very appetizing. And I don't even like beer. I pour myself a full pint and chug down half of it in one go.

The pizzas arrive just before the guys join us. Jace raises his eyebrows at me in question when he sees me drinking beer.

He slides in next to me. "You don't have to drink beer, you know?"

I glare at him. "Of course I know that, Jace." What? Does he think I've changed too, like Dorothy suggested? "I'm not a peer pressure victim, don't worry." I'm just trying to cope with the anxiety of seeing two girls who seem out to get me sitting together twenty feet away.

Jace slides his arm around me. "Don't be mad at me." He kisses the top of my head and I sink into him. "How was practice?" he asks.

I stiffen, remembering the conversation with Coach. I came here to avoid thinking about track. "Fine."

Jace turns to look at me, tucking a stray hair behind my ear. His phone alerts him to an incoming text message at the same time that I feel a buzz from mine in my back pocket.

Unlocking my phone, I open a picture text from an unknown number. It's a couple making out on the hood of a Jeep. Ryan's Jeep. The girl sits on the hood, her arms around his neck, and Ryan's hands are under her shirt, on her hips. Frowning, I peer closer. It's a brunette, and definitely not Lisa. The message below says, *Cheaters*.

My eyes bug out when I recognize the purple Converse sneakers wrapped around Ryan's waist.

"What the fuck?" Jace growls.

When I glance up, everyone is staring at their phones. Except for Lisa, who is staring at me. Her face is beet red, and she looks like she's going to claw my eyes out. I look around for Ryan, to help me explain, but he must still be at practice.

"That picture, it must be from a long time ago," I say quickly.

Jace's hands are clenching and unclenching on the table. I put my hand on top of his, trying to soothe him, but he yanks his fist away.

"I think Madeline sent it," I say quietly. Lisa shoots out of her seat, ready to bolt.

Kayla grabs her arm and pulls her back down. "Don't. You're just giving her what she wants."

"I swear, you guys. This photo is from months ago," I try to explain.

"Why the hell would someone bother taking a photo of the two of you back then? And why save it? That doesn't make a whole lot of fucking sense, Pepper," Lisa growls at me. She's right. It's super weird.

"I have no idea." That's all I can say. It's really creepy that someone was watching us during that private moment. It was at the park by the high school, and we thought we were alone.

Our phones beep simultaneously and I swallow hard before looking at the message.

It's in the hallway by the locker rooms and we're wearing running clothes. Ryan's head is leaning down to kiss my neck. Jace's favorite place to kiss. Before I can try to explain, Jace grabs my hand and pulls me roughly out of the booth. It's all I can do to keep up with him as he barrels through the restaurant. I refuse to look at Madeline's table, but I notice other kids from Brockton Public gawking at us.

He pushes me roughly up against the back of his Jeep, away from the prying eyes at the restaurant. His green eyes are ablaze and I can feel his chest rising and falling against mine.

"Pepper," he says with a croak. The pain in his voice cuts into me. I shake my head back and forth. No, Jace. You can't believe it.

"When were those photos taken?"

"In the fall, Jace. Before we were together," I spill the words out.

The tension in his face, in his stance, relaxes considerably. "Has anyone touched you besides me since we've been together?" he asks in a softer voice.

"No. I hardly even talk to Ryan. That time at my apartment is the only time I've really talked to him for more than a minute since we broke up."

Jace's body sags into mine and he brushes his thumb along my cheekbone. "I believe you." He presses his mouth roughly to mine, as if trying to show me through a kiss that he trusts me.

When he breaks away, he leans his forehead against mine. "I trust you, Pep, you know I do. And I know there are people trying to come between us. It's just really hard for me to think rationally when I see..." He clenches his jaw and closes his eyes. "I can't look at those fucking photos again. Delete them from my phone. Please."

"I will," I whisper, slipping the phone out of his pocket and putting it in mine.

A car door slams and Jace turns around quickly to see Ryan jogging toward us. "I take it you got the messages too?" I ask when I see the confusion and distress in his eyes.

"Yeah," he quickly glances to Jace. "You know those are from months ago, right? Before you guys" – he gestures between us – "got together."

"I know, man. But I still don't want to fucking look at you right now. Sorry. You might want to head inside and talk to your girlfriend." Jace's voice has returned to a controlled, unemotional tone, but I know it's taking a lot for him to rein it in. He knows Ryan didn't do anything wrong, but he's never been especially rational when it comes to me.

Jace's grip on the steering wheel on the drive home tells me he's still shaken. He turns up the radio, blocking out any conversation.

When we turn onto a street out of town, I look over at Jace. "Where are we going?" I'm nearly shouting over the music.

"I'm taking you out to dinner. You didn't get a chance to eat."

Jace brings us to a little pub in Alpine, a small neighboring town. He doesn't want to deal with running into anyone from Brockton.

We order burgers, and eat in comfortable silence, sitting side by side in the booth. He steals my fries, and I let him.

When we're both stuffed and leaning back in our seats, I tell Jace, "I have a feeling this is only the beginning."

He takes my hand and rubs small circles on the palm. "You're probably right. But we've got something that they don't understand. Yeah, it pisses me off to see those photos, but I trust you, Pep. I know you."

I squeeze his hand. His voice wavers a little, and I wonder how true those words are. If pushed hard enough, can that trust be broken?

He raises our hands to his lips and gives my knuckles a hard kiss. "I wish I could take back a lot of the stupid shit I did before," he says.

That *would* be nice.

"What took us so long to be together, anyway?" I ask.

He smirks at me, and I wiggle in my seat. No one can smirk like Jace Wilder. It's a huge turn-on.

"You weren't ready for me, Pep."

I tug my hand away and cross my arms. "What? I think you mean *you* weren't ready for *me*. I didn't have a single boyfriend until this year and you" – I wave my hand in his direction – "were with girls all the time. Then, as soon as I get my first boyfriend, you decide you're ready for me. What's up with that, huh?"

Jace tries to contain his laughter at my outburst but I see through it. My eyes narrow and I shove him in the chest.

"Okay, okay." He raises his hand in defeat. "I didn't want to mess things up with you. How many times do I have to tell you? You're special, Pep. Too good for me, or anyone. I didn't want to give something a try and fuck it all up and lose you."

My head tilts to the side as I take this in. And then I smirk right back at him. "You" – I point at his chest – "big bad Jace Wilder. Were afraid of losing me" – I point to myself with a huge grin on my face – "little Pepper Jones, the girl next door?"

He grabs my finger and pulls me toward him so that I'm almost sitting on his lap. "I'm still scared," he whispers gruffly.

Jace's head dips lower, nuzzling my neck. His warm breath sends goose bumps along my spine as his lips skim my jaw line. "Terrified, actually."

A confession like this from Jace doesn't come often. But he's getting better at sharing his feelings with me. Well, some of his feelings. I still haven't gotten much from him about Annie.

Our phones continue buzzing throughout the night, and we distract ourselves by starting a challenging jigsaw puzzle at Jace's house. Puzzles have always been one of our favorite things to do together.

I scroll through Jace's phone before heading home for the night, deleting the photo messages. Several more came through of me and Ryan together, but all of them are from the fall. It means a lot that Jace trusts me enough to delete all of them without even looking at them himself. But I can understand the motivation to avoid having those images seared in his brain.

***

People stare at me when I walk into school the next day. Zoe warned me what to expect earlier that morning. Everyone knows about the photos. No surprise there. Until word gets around that Jace doesn't believe I cheated on him – that the photos were from the fall – I have to deal with hostile glares.

But I don't anticipate the lovely decorations greeting me at my locker. The word "slut" is written in big black letters. It's definitely a girl who did this because the bold writing is very neat. The photos that were texted last night have been printed out – in color, no less – and are taped all over my locker.

I would rip all the photos off but I prefer not to give the crowd gathering behind me that satisfaction. Instead, I pretend I don't care. Stoically, I turn my locker combination, desperately trying to wipe any signs of humiliation from my face. With shaky hands, I grab the books I need for the entire day so I don't have to come back to my locker. My backpack weighs at least 50 pounds but I really don't care.

I spin around and pause to narrow my eyes at the growing crowd in the hallway before heading to first period. It's going to be a long day.

Chapter 14

Ryan catches me in the halls between first and second period.

"Pepper, I need your help." He takes my arm and pulls me into an empty classroom.

"Ryan, being alone in a classroom right now is a bad idea. More rumors are the last thing we need." I don't mean to sound so angry, but it's a stupid move on his part and I'm sure people saw us go in here.

"Sorry," he says, cringing. "It's just, I thought it'd be worse trying to have a private conversation with you in the hallway."

"Yeah, I get it. So, what's up?" I wonder if his locker was vandalized as well. Doubtful. I'm pretty sure this was meant to be an attack on me. Or me and Jace. Ryan is just a casualty.

"Can you talk to Lisa? Explain that those photos are from months ago?" Ryan shoves his hands in his pockets and looks at his feet. Why won't he make eye contact with me?

"She doesn't believe you?"

"I think she wants to, but she kept calling all night asking questions about each photo. She won't let it go."

"I can try, if you think it will help." It probably won't.

"Thanks, Pepper," he says with relief.

"Who do you think took them?" I have my suspicions, but maybe he has different ones.

"I have no idea. It's really weirding me out though. Who do you think would stalk us like that?"

"I think it could have been Dorothy," I say quietly.

Ryan's eyes widen. "That's crazy. Why?"

"Just a feeling." There's no time to elaborate. "Come on, we should get to second period before more rumors start rolling."

When we leave the classroom, Remy and Jace are standing in the hallway with their arms crossed. The rest of the hallway is empty, and I know we're all going to be late for class. But as my eyes lock with Jace's, that's the least of my concern.

"Are you trying to make this harder on me for some reason?" he asks after a long silence. I hear Remy speaking angrily to Ryan as they round the corner down the hall.

Shaking my head, I approach Jace slowly and touch his arm. His voice is hard, and he's masking his emotion. But I know that's when he's closest to snapping.

"He just wanted me to talk to Lisa. That's all. I'm sorry it looked sketchy."

Jace runs a hand over his face and looks away. His body is rigid, and I want to hug him until he relaxes in my arms. Instead, I keep my hand resting on his forearm, feeling the muscles tense underneath my fingertips.

I can't force him to trust me.

"This is one of so many reasons why I never wanted us to be more than friends."

My heart drops to my stomach at his words. "What?" I choke out.

His green eyes dart back to my face and his features soften. "You, more than anyone, can hurt me." He steps into me, closing the space between us.

"Try not to break my fucking heart, okay?" he says as he kisses my temple.

I smile with relief. "I'll try not to break your fucking heart," I promise.

Jace makes it clear that everything's good with us by sitting me on his lap during lunch period. The mean glares diminish significantly for the rest of the afternoon, making me thankful for Jace's influence over the student population.

Jace assures me that my locker will be clean by tomorrow. I don't know how that's possible, because it looked like permanent marker, but I trust him.

***

By Saturday morning, the drama with the photo texts and locker is far from my mind. I'm a bundle of nerves as Zoe parks the family minivan outside Hutchinson High. I'm sitting in the back row with Rollie. Ryan and Claire are in the middle seats and Charlie has shotgun. I watch my teammates pile out, but I'm reluctant to move from the safety of the van.

Parents and athletes are everywhere. Hutchinson High has some of the best sports facilities in the state and they are hosting a big tennis tournament and a track meet on the same day.

It'll be my first individual race since I won Nationals. I've avoided Googling myself but I've heard my name mentioned a couple times on the local news this week. Thankfully, Ryan has already raced some fast times this year, and he's getting a lot more attention. They're still referring to us as the "Brockton High

Phenomena". It's not a title I'm comfortable with.

Charlie pokes his head in the sliding door. "You coming?"

"Do I have to?" I mumble as I make my way outside.

Charlie throws an arm around my shoulder. "It's a beautiful day for a track meet. You've done this a million times. Just race like you always do."

"Yeah, yeah," I grumble as I swing my track bag over my shoulder. I am so not feeling it.

Fortunately, there are so many different events at track meets that it takes the focus away from my race. I make an effort to cheer for my teammates in their events, and it distracts me from my own race. But I can't kick the anxiety weighing me down. The mile is one of the last races of the day and I can't wait for it to be over with.

Claire and Jenny are racing the mile as well and we jog around the high school together to warm up. Claire's a senior and is headed to some engineering college on the east coast next year. They have a decent Division III running program, and she plans to race. School's always been her first priority though.

Jenny is only a freshman but she's a super-talented runner. This is her first time racing the mile. She might actually give me some competition. Sometimes I find her right on my heels at practice.

My eyes flicker to Dorothy as we run by the tennis courts. She's filling up a water bottle and when she catches me watching she smirks and raises a single, perfectly-shaped eyebrow. I've never been able to raise one eyebrow like that, but if it makes everyone look as evil as Dorothy, then I'm okay not having that special ability.

We sit down on the grass by the pole vault to stretch and put on our "spikes" – lightweight sneakers with little spikes on the bottom. I have the same hot pink pair that I raced in last year. I'll probably need a new pair soon. For some reason, most track spikes come in bright colors. As I rummage through my track bag, I don't spot any hot pink. I dump the contents out and sure enough, my track spikes are missing.

I know I packed them. I always pack my bag the night before, and my spikes and uniform are the first things that go in it. The race starts in five minutes. I've got just enough time to run over to the van to see if they are in there.

"Where's Zoe?" I ask the girls impatiently. "I need her car keys."

We all look around but don't see her. I spot her track bag and frantically sort through it, feeling for the keys. When I find them, I sprint over to the parking lot. I usually do a couple of short sprints as part of my warm-up, so this will have to suffice. It'd be great to miss the race, but I don't want to deal with the questions that will follow if I do. It would only increase the buildup for my next individual race.

After searching under the van seats and in the trunk, I come up empty. Ugh! I guess I'm racing in my regular sneakers. It's not the end of the world, but it will definitely slow me down. Not to mention, it just feels weird. Okay, I also admit it bothers me that I'll look really silly. Wearing a sleek track uniform and regular running shoes is a totally awkward look. Very amateur. I have no choice but to rock it.

When I get to the track, the first heat for the mile has already finished and they are lining up for the second one. Based on my seed time, I'm number one, so they call my name first. I'm breathing heavily when I jog over, and people are giving me funny looks. Whether it's because I look like I already ran the race or because I'm not wearing track spikes, I don't know.

There are a lot of people in this heat, which means it's going to be important to get well-positioned right from the start. I've gotten myself locked on the inside and behind lots of people before, and it's pretty frustrating.

"Runners, take your marks!" I crouch into position. Boom! The gun goes off and I shoot forward, but not fast enough. Without spikes to grip the track as I push off, several other runners quickly move ahead of me.

My feet feel sluggish as we turn the first corner, but I'm mostly concentrating on all the bodies around me and them breathing down my neck. The first lap of the mile is always like this – utter chaos. That's because, unlike the shorter races, we don't have assigned lanes.

It's really hard to control the pace on the first lap. Sometimes it's way too fast, and sometimes it's way too slow. Right now, it seems too fast, but maybe it's because I don't have spikes on.

By the time we come around the first lap, the pack has thinned out enough that I don't have to worry about tripping and falling. There are four girls in front of me, including Jenny. I usually try to be in the front of the front pack –

not setting the pace but in second or third. That way I don't have to break the wind but I can easily move ahead when I'm ready. I'm further back than usual, but I'm just not feeling especially aggressive at the moment.

Coaches yell our splits as we run through the first lap, and as I suspected, we've gone out way too fast. We're on pace to break five minutes, which I seriously doubt anyone will actually do today. The pace immediately eases up slightly when we hear the split; I'm not the only one who knows it'll be brutal if we try to keep it up.

I decide to stay where I am and let people fall back as they get worn out. This is often a smart approach, but today I know I'm doing it for the wrong reasons. I don't want to test myself. I'm not submitting control of the race because it's smart race tactics – even if it is. I should just be running my own race, because winning it shouldn't be too much of a challenge.

But the last thing I want is to go out too hard and not be able to follow through. Slowing down at the end of a race or getting passed by someone is my worst nightmare. It's a good fear to have as a cross country runner, because the races are longer. But it's not ideal for racing the mile. Still, I'd much prefer to race conservatively and finish strong. Even if it means I'm being a chicken.

When we head into our fourth and final lap, it looks like there are five of us in the top pack. We've settled into a decent pace – fast enough to qualify for State – but unless I really drop the hammer, I'm not going to be impressing anyone today.

I can hear the commentator speculating about when I'll take off. I'm not feeling especially drained, and I should really start picking it up. If I wait until the last minute to sprint, someone else might outsprint me.

Reluctantly, I move out into the second lane and pick off the girls in front of me one by one. Normally, I love this part of the race. But the adrenaline rush I'm expecting never comes.

I'm in front now, and it's liberating. I'm not feeling the typical burn that hits me at this point, but for some reason my legs will not go any faster. They feel heavy and soft. There's someone on my shoulder and I just can't seem to go any faster to brush them off.

"Pepper Jones and Jenny Mendoza have left the lead pack in the dust as they round this last curve. It's a Brockton Public race to the finish!"

I grit my teeth and lift my knees higher in an effort to urge my body into sprint mode. I know the stupid shoe situation isn't helping, but it's more than that. My body will not cooperate!

There's no doubt Jenny's suffering by the sound of her labored breathing. I'm barely breaking a sweat. Pumping my arms, I finally get my legs to engage in a half-hearted sprint. Jenny quickly falls back and I move ahead to take the win with a few seconds to spare. It's a relief to avoid embarrassment, but it's not exactly a race to be proud of.

My time – 5:15 – isn't what people expect from the national cross country champion.

Stuffing down my feelings, I congratulate Jenny on her awesome race and State qualifying time. Claire's pleased as well, having hit the District qualifying time. Zoe joins us for a warm-down jog – it's a warm-up for her next race – and I listen to the girls dissect the mile.

They tell me how much faster I would have been if I had my spikes, but I know that's not the main reason I didn't have a good race. I'll let them believe that excuse for now. It's too hard to explain what's going on when I don't understand it myself.

As we jog by the parking lot, I notice an object sitting on the hood of Zoe's van. Two hot pink objects, to be precise.

"What the?" Picking up my pace, I run toward the van.

Sure enough, my spikes are sitting on the hood. With a sign in front of them that says "slut." How original.

I hear the girls murmuring behind me.

"Who do you think would do this?" Claire asks. "Everyone likes you."

"Not everyone," I say through clenched teeth. This is petty and ridiculous but it's getting its intended effect. I'm angry. Hurt. Annoyed. Embarrassed. And definitely on edge about what's coming next.

"It was Dorothy!" Zoe exclaims. "I knew it! She's always been jealous of you, Pepper. And did you know the tennis team is here today? She totally took those photos of you and Ryan in the fall and was hoping to have an opportunity to use them."

Zoe is pacing and throwing her arms in the air.

"What a schemer!" she exclaims.

"We should do something to get back at her," Jenny says with a nod.

"I'm kind of hoping if I just ignore her it will go away," I tell them.

"Fat chance," Zoe says with a huff. She snags the sign off the hood and rips it up before throwing it in a nearby trash can.

I grab my spikes and carry them while we jog back to the track.

"You really aren't going to do anything about this?" Zoe asks.

"Like what?"

"I don't know. Let's come up with a prank. It'll be fun!"

"You don't really want to go there, do you? Stoop to her level? Besides, I'm pretty sure she's doing this under Madeline Brescoll's direction."

"Madeline Brescoll? Why?" Claire asks.

"Madeline wants Jace," Zoe explains.

"Even I know to avoid messing with Madeline Brescoll," Jenny says. "Half of the freshman girls idolize her and half are terrified of her."

"She doesn't even go to our school," Claire reflects. "Who cares about her?"

"The Barbies care," I tell them. "They were anticipating something like this, and they seemed almost excited about it. They want to shut her down. Show her they're more powerful or something."

"You should tell them about your spikes," Zoe says. "That will help fire them up. Don't want nobody messing with our Brockton High Phenomenon." She nudges me in the ribs.

"Don't call me that," I say moodily. "And I'm not telling them. Let's keep it on the DL."

"DL?" Claire asks.

"Down low," Jenny says, indulging our nerdy friend with an explanation.

As we near the track, I spot Lisa and Andrea walking away from the tennis courts and toward the locker room doors. This might be my only opportunity to talk to Lisa about the photos.

"I need to talk to Lisa about something, guys, I'll be back in a few." More drama is the last thing I need right now, but I need to do this for Ryan.

I reach the girls as they open the door to the high school.

"Hey, um, Lisa, I was hoping I could talk to you. Do you have a couple of minutes?"

Lisa crosses her arms. "What do you want to talk about?"

Andrea saves me from responding. "We just finished our matches so we're hanging out waiting on the rest of the games. You two go chat," she says with a wave of her hand.

"Why don't you come with?" Lisa asks her.

Andrea raises her eyebrows in question to me.

I shrug. "Sure." It might be good to have a third person there.

As we make our way to a bench in the empty hallway, I turn to Lisa. "I just wanted to explain to you that those photos are from months ago."

"That's what Ryan said too. But some of the photos look recent, Pepper. Care to explain that?"

I hadn't spent much time looking at them.

Andrea takes out her phone and hands it to Lisa. "Here, show her why you think so."

We sit down on the bench and I end up sandwiched between them, the photo of Ryan and me kissing in our running clothes shoved in front of me.

"See? You guys are wearing hats and are covered in snow. We didn't get snow like that in the fall."

Frowning, I try to remember when this happened. Ryan and I weren't exactly kissing in public all the time, and this must have been after one of the practices in December, when everyone else was done with their season and we were training for Nationals together. Because it was early December, most fall sports were over and we could get away with a kiss by the locker rooms without an audience.

"It was in December," I explain to Lisa. "Our season went later than everyone else's because of Nationals. We had some snow one afternoon."

I glance at her and she seems to accept my answer. She scrolls to the next one. Ryan and I are lying on the grass, and my head is on his chest. "See that Spanish book opened next to Ryan? He just started taking Spanish this semester."

Suppressing my smile, I tell her, "I take Spanish. That's my book."

She scrolls through a couple more photos, pointing out the length of his haircut or an outfit as evidence that the photo was taken more recently. Eventually, she gives up.

"Okay, now I feel stupid," she says with a laugh. "I'll stop now."

I sigh with relief, happy that someone else's relationship isn't going to get messed up because of me.

"Sorry I've been such a bitch to you, Pepper," Lisa says quietly. "It's just, I've liked Ryan since he moved here and, well, he picked you first. Which sucked."

"That's okay. I mean, I get why you didn't want to like me. You haven't been mean or anything."

Andrea giggles at that.

"What? She hasn't. Just not super nice, that's all. Whoever sent these photos is mean. Big difference."

"Don't worry," Andrea says. "If they want to play this game, we'll play. Kayla's already got some ideas up her sleeves."

"What do you mean? You know who did this?" I ask.

Andrea gives me a doubtful look. "Come on, there aren't many people obsessed enough to get these photos, save them, and use them. Dorothy Sandoval has been scheming to be friends with us since junior high. Who knows what she originally had planned when she took these photos? But I can't think of anyone else weird enough to do it."

"What about Madeline?" I ask.

"She's the reason Dorothy sent them. Dorothy must have given up on being our friend since we're graduating soon, and figured she'd try to get in with Madeline's group instead," Lisa says.

"They're just using her," Andrea adds.

"I'm sure she knows that. She seems to be enjoying herself, though," I say bitterly, remembering the smirk she gave me earlier today.

"We'll deal with her," Andrea says as we make our way back outside.

"Well, it's Pepper this was aimed at. Maybe Pepper wants to be involved," Lisa says.

"No, I really don't." I'm thankful to have the opportunity to make that clear. Still, I'm not about to get on my high horse and try to talk them out of retaliating. I have a feeling it won't do any good anyway.

Chapter 15

After the meet, Zoe drives us over to Brockton Public to catch the tail end of a home baseball game. I see Jim sitting with his girlfriend Sheila on one side and Annie and Helen on the other, so we grab an empty row in the bleachers behind them and between innings I introduce them to my friends.

With a hot dog in one hand and a Coke in the other, I'm able to relax and momentarily forget about the attack that's been launched against me by Madeline and Dorothy.

Jace glances my way when he steps up to the plate and I can't help grinning like a fool. The dirt-streaked uniform emphasizes his athletic build. He looks intimidating as he grips the bat, and it contrasts with the soft, knowing smile he gives me. I'm filled with a rush of adoration for this boy, who loves me unconditionally.

It doesn't come as a surprise that he's the star of the game. I feel a distinct sense of pride when he hits a grand slam.

Jace is in a great mood after the game. It's strange watching him with Annie and Jim. He looks happy, and they are both so proud of him. I hate the ugly tug of emotion in my gut. It's not jealousy, because I'm happy for Jace.

But it hurts. I guess it's always comforted me that my best friend shared a loss like me. Now he has a complete family. Even a brother.

The dark feelings quickly evaporate when he picks me up and swings me around. His good mood is contagious.

"Let's get you home to shower. I'm cooking you dinner tonight," he announces.

"Oh?" Jace can cook breakfast, but I've never seen him cook dinner. "Let me guess. Breakfast for dinner?"

"You'll just have to wait and see," he says before kissing me and setting me down.

"Are you saying I stink? Maybe I want to come over now and I don't want a shower."

"You always smell good, Pep. I swear, it's like an ocean smell or something." He nestles his head in my neck and inhales.

"You know, you said that once before, but you were kind of messed up at the time." It was back in the fall when he'd been rolling on ecstasy and Wes had convinced me he needed an intervention. I'm so glad he didn't continue down that path. That time feels very long ago.

It's almost three hours later when I finally make it to Jace's. Gran talked me into getting a pedicure with her, and Jace said he still had to run to the grocery store anyway.

I walk down the street to his place with a couple of movies and a puzzle. I've got on my favorite pair of yoga pants, a cotton tee shirt, and flip flops. Jace and I have had many nights like this over the years, but it's so much better now that he's my boyfriend. I love the intimacies we can share now – like cuddling during a movie, or a kiss to celebrate finding the right puzzle piece.

Jace's house is dark when I open the front door and kick off my flip flops.

"Jace?" I call out.

Frowning, I start to walk up the stairs toward the kitchen. I nearly tumble back down when the lights switch on and a dozen familiar voices shout, "SURPRISE!"

Loud music blares and confetti fills the air around me. I'm still clutching my chest and trying to breathe when Jace picks me up for a kiss. "It's an early birthday party." I turn seventeen in a few days.

I can't stop smiling as I take in the streamers and decorations. "You did all this?"

"I had some help," he tells me. Looking at those familiar green eyes, I can't help the wetness filling my own.

"Hey, don't cry." Jace wipes the tears away.

I sniff. "I don't know why I'm crying. They're happy tears." I laugh when I hear Katy Perry. "Nice tunes, Jace. Was Zoe in charge of the music?"

He smiles sheepishly. "Well, I know how much you like your girly music."

"Stop stealing the birthday girl, Jace!" Zoe pulls me in for a hug and hands me a glass of champagne.

Wesley is the next to lift me in a bear hug before I'm passed around like a teddy bear.

All my buddies are here – Jenny, Claire, Rollie, Charlie and Omar. Jace's friends, who I guess are also my friends now, greet me with hugs too – Remy, Connor, Ben, and even Ryan. The Barbies are dolled up, as usual, but my lack of appropriate attire doesn't faze me. Lisa must have come around at the last minute, after our conversation this afternoon.

It's awesome to have everyone together like this. They have me and Jace in common, and without other people around, it's easy to ignore the social classifications that normally divide us.

As the night goes on, I'm impressed with the excellent selection of music. Jace proudly admits to his friends that he is responsible for the mix that includes all of my favorites – Rihanna, Taylor Swift, Lady Gaga. The guys give him a hard time, but it only makes the girls crush on him harder. One girl in particular. I am so crazy about him.

Jace lied about cooking, but he ordered plenty of pizza and I'm not complaining. Claire even baked a cake. I couldn't have asked for a better seventeenth birthday party.

Jace is attentive, but less possessive than he is at the bigger parties. He knows I know everyone here, and that I'm comfortable. It's nice not to worry about the likes of Madeline Brescoll showing up, or to deal with people I don't know constantly seeking Jace's attention.

I'm really able to let my guard down.

There's an awkward moment when Zoe lets it slip that she calls Kayla, Andrea and Lisa the Barbies, but she manages to smooth it over. Zoe explains that they are just so beautiful and since they're all blonde, it's a fitting title. Only Zoe can turn an insult into a compliment. And now she's bonding with her new friends, her arms slung around Andrea's and Kayla's shoulders as they sway back and forth singing "Here's my number, so call me maybe," at the top of their lungs.

Even Claire has loosened up. And Jenny, only a freshman, doesn't seem the least bit intimidated by the Barbies. I drag Jace up from the couch to dance with me, and pretty soon the girls have gotten all the boys to join in our dance party.

Apparently no one has to worry about driving because Jace told people ahead of time they can crash at his house.

It's two in the morning when the energy starts to wind down. I guess I can be a bossy drunk because I demand that everyone get into their pajamas so that I'm not the only one in mine.

"You sure you want me in mine? You know I only sleep in my underwear, Pep," Jace says softly in my ear.

"I think I'm ready for bed anyway," I tell him, turning to snuggle into his arms. I've tried not to give in to my urge to be in his arms all night so that I can spend time with everyone else. But I'm really looking forward to being alone with him.

"All right, party people," Jace announces. "The birthday girl is ready for bed. Find any couch or floor space to crash on." He scoops me up and carries me downstairs as our friends cheer and whoop.

"Are they going to be okay on the floor? I can send people to my apartment."

"I knew you'd be concerned about everyone else, so I told them ahead of time to bring sleeping bags. We've got it covered, Pep, don't worry."

Jace plops me on his bed and places kisses along my legs as he takes off my yoga pants. I prop up on my elbows to watch him as he takes his own pants and shirt off.

"Are you tired?" he asks softly.

"No," I whisper. And judging by the smoldering look in his eyes, he likes my answer.

Jace pulls my hips to the edge of the bed and settles onto his knees. He gently kisses my stomach, and I continue watching him as he slowly slides my underwear down my legs. He's never touched me there before. I'm completely exposed. But I don't feel shy. I trust Jace like no one else.

"I'm going to make sure you don't forget this birthday, Pep. Are you ready to feel really good?" he asks, his hand gently massaging my inner thighs but not touching my most private place.

I nod, wide-eyed. He reaches to move a pillow behind my head. "Just relax," he instructs. I let my head fall back as I give myself over to Jace's caresses.

My eyes drift closed and I simply let myself feel every wonderful sensation. Is it possible to be any happier?

***

The rest of the weekend is just as blissful. Except when Jace asks about my race, and I'm reminded about the spikes-stealing incident. I hate keeping things from him but he'll just get angry and it's not an embarrassment I want to rehash.

Jim stayed out with Sheila and we have the house to ourselves Sunday morning. Jace and Wes team up to make everyone pancakes. After a short jog with Dave, I meet Jace at a park with Annie and some friends she's made since she moved back. It's kind of strange playing Frisbee and grilling burgers with people twenty years older than us. They act like we're just their buddies, not kids.

My bias against Annie starts to break down when she stops by my house later that week after my birthday dinner with Gran and Jace. It's a Wednesday night, so we keep the celebration low-key.

Gran hasn't seen Annie since she returned. Annie actually breaks down crying when Gran gives her a hug. When she declines the alcoholic beverage Gran offers, Gran is not shy asking about her addiction recovery.

"So, what exactly were you addicted to, dear?"

Annie can't hide the small smile at Gran's boldness. "Oh, just about anything I could get my hands on. It changed for periods of time depending on what was available, who I was hanging with. I kept moving to new towns, thinking if I got away from the people I used with that I could stop. But it would start all over again."

I glance at Jace, curious how much of this the two of them have already discussed. His expression doesn't give anything away but he takes my hand and squeezes.

Gran nods. "You look a lot better than you did at 25, or however old you were when I last saw you."

"Thanks. I feel better too." She looks down at her hands. "I wish it hadn't taken me so long to get here, but I'm glad I'm back."

"Well, let's make sure you stay then," Gran says sternly. "Are you in a recovery group or seeing a counselor?"

"I go to NA meetings. Narcotics Anonymous," she clarifies. "And Helen's been really great. She was one of my only sober friends in college. And she's been real supportive."

Before heading home, Annie hands me a wrapped gift. It's a double frame with two photos of Jace and me. One is crumpled and worn, but it's me as a little girl, with my face covered in chocolate ice cream. Jace is trying to lick it off my cheek and I'm laughing. The photo next to it was taken on Saturday after the game. Jace has lifted me off my feet and we're grinning at each other. We look totally in love.

"I'm sorry the older one isn't in great shape. I've had it for a very long time," Annie says nervously.

"Thank you, Annie. This is a really amazing gift." I try to convey gratitude in my voice. When I give her a hug, my gaze catches Jace's from the door. His eyes are filled with some deep emotion that I can't identify. I've never seen him look so moved.

He walks out with Annie after giving me and Gran kisses on the cheek.

When Annie showed up at the Wilders' back in February, I never could have predicted this is how things would work out. It's not what I expected, but it doesn't matter. Jace has never been so content. The turmoil that's always simmering deep in him has disappeared.

I notice Gran's cheeks are wet when I give her a hug on my way to my bedroom. She feels it too.

Chapter 16

It shouldn't surprise me that Dorothy takes it upon herself to ensure that my blissful state doesn't last too long.

"Oh, hi Pepper," she says dismissively, as though she didn't purposefully plant herself in front of my locker on Monday morning.

"What do you want, Dorothy?"

"I heard you didn't quite have it on Saturday in the mile." She looks down at her nails before flicking her eyes up to gauge my reaction.

I stare her down, refusing to give a response.

"You know, you wouldn't have to deal with inconveniences like misplacing your spikes if you just ended things with Jace. He's going to college soon and it's not going to last. You might as well save yourself some trouble." She smirks. "Because there's bound to be trouble."

"I'm not going to break up with Jace, Dorothy. So just give it up." I try to say it like her threats are meaningless. But if she could feel my heart rate, she'd know I'm worried. If it was only Dorothy I was dealing with, it'd be different. But Madeline is behind this.

"You should just let him enjoy some freedom for the rest of his senior year. He will anyway. But why make him feel guilty about it?" She shrugs before spinning around and walking away.

I turn to my locker, but I'm so distracted that I find myself fumbling with the lock. Dorothy's getting to me. What are they going to come up with next to mess with me and Jace? He's so happy right now; why do these girls have to put that in jeopardy?

I feel warm breath on my neck and watch tan hands take mine and move them away from my lock. His body is pressed warmly against my back as he turns my lock and opens it on the first try. I turn around, captured between his arms.

"Thanks."

"What was Dorothy talking to you about?" Jace asks. His jaw clenches as he grips my hips and tugs me flush against him.

I avoid his question. "She's probably the one who sent those photos. You know that, right?"

He nods.

"I guess she's doing Madeline's dirty work. Trying to tell me worse things will come if I don't just break up with you." Rolling my eyes, I turn to my locker to get my books. He's scrutinizing me and I don't want him to know how much her words worried me.

"Let me handle her." His voice is gentle but stern.

"Who? Madeline or Dorothy?"

"Both. I thought I'd sent Madeline a pretty clear message already, but apparently not," he says tightly.

"Don't do anything yet, Jace. Kayla's already planning to mess with Dorothy, and I don't want to turn this into a bigger thing than it is." I don't want to think about how crazy it could get if Jace gets involved. He's never handled things subtly. Talk about disturbing our peaceful happy place.

He narrows his eyes. "I'll talk to Kayla. Maybe it's best if the girls handle it for now."

I kiss him lightly on the lips for agreeing with me.

"Wes is throwing a party on Saturday. Will you be up for it after your meet? The meet's up in the mountains, right? You might not get back until late."

"I can come by," I tell him. He takes my hand as we walk toward class.

"He wants you there. It's going to be a big one. But if you're exhausted, it's no problem. I'll come by to hang out with you."

"Hang out?" I flutter my eyelashes, remembering the way Saturday night ended.

"Or something..." he says with a sexy smirk.

"That's not going to help motivate me to go to Wes's, Jace."

We pause in front of my classroom.

"You know it means a lot to Wes that you're friends with him again. I feel pretty shitty that you guys stopped hanging for so long because of me," Jace confesses.

"Well, it's not like Wes didn't play a part. He dropped me. I wasn't even put in a position of having to choose."

Jace's eyes darken and his forehead creases at my remark.

I tilt me head at his disturbed expression. "You know I would have chosen you, if it came to it," I tease.

"Not a joking matter, Pep." Holding my chin, he kisses me on the head and pats my butt before nudging me into class.

***

This time when we arrive at the track meet, I don't feel nervous. In fact, I don't feel much at all about racing the 2-mile today. I'm rather indifferent. Apathetic.

Because the meet's far away, we travel as a team in a school bus. I do my homework on the way there while most of my teammates fall back to sleep. I like getting assignments out of the way so I can spend more time with Jace on the weekends. Although he has actually been doing his homework with me more often these days. It's an odd time to start caring about school, given that he's about to graduate and already has a college athletic scholarship. I wonder if Annie being around has anything to do with it.

The clouds in the sky threaten rain as Zoe and I warm up for the 2-mile. I usually race my best in cooler weather like this. Maybe my lack of nervousness will help me race better. I'm trying to stay positive, but there's an icky feeling brewing about this race that I can't ignore.

The tennis team isn't playing here, so at least I don't have to worry about my spikes getting stolen.

The 2-mile is one of the first races of the day. Ryan's racing it as well, and he and Charlie jog up next to us during our warm up run. As Charlie and Zoe chat about something, Ryan says quietly, "Hey, I haven't had a chance to thank you for talking to Lisa."

"Oh, she told you about that?"

"She didn't say much about your conversation, but she hasn't questioned me about the photos since."

"You know, Ryan, I was hoping maybe we could start hanging out and being friends more, but I have a feeling we won't be able to get away with that now. At least not for a little while."

I glance at him from the corner of my eye, curious for his reaction. He flashes a dimpled smile, telling me he's happy I'm hoping we can be closer again in the future. Even if we have to put it on hold for now. I think that my relationship with Jace is strong enough to withstand Ryan and me being friends, but it's not worth the gossip that will inevitably follow in light of the recent photo texts.

"I'd like that, Pepper," he says. "I've missed you. As a friend, I mean," he quickly clarifies.

We pass Coach, who calls Zoe and me over while the boys continue on their warm-up run.

"You remember Kendra Smith?" Coach asks me.

"The name sounds familiar. Didn't she win State?" The State cross meet was a bit of a disaster race for me this past fall, but I managed to get by just enough to qualify for the next big race – Regionals – thanks to Jenny who gave up her qualifying spot.

"Yup. Great runner. She usually runs a sound race. I saw she's seeded right behind you today in the 2-mile. It'd be smart to just settle in with her and let her set the pace."

I like the sound of that. I won't have to think about much.

"Unless she's really off pace, then you'll probably need to run your own race. I don't think there will be anyone else for you to run with."

Coach moves on to talk to Zoe about her race. Zoe is trying to qualify for State too, but she'll be a ways behind me. She qualified last year and I bet she'll do it again, but it's not as much of a sure thing as it is for me.

As we approach the start line, Zoe points out Kendra Smith. I recognize her from cross country. She has the same body type as me – a little taller than most distance runners and long legs. We both have long brown hair pulled back in ponytails. Her school colors are purple and her running spikes, socks and hairband match the uniform.

She smiles hesitantly my way when she catches me eyeing her.

I return her smile, slightly embarrassed. Maybe I'll get a chance to talk to her after the race. Maybe I'll even thank her for setting the pace for me. If she sets a good pace, that is. Actually, if I beat her, that would be sort of obnoxious.

The first lap is slow – too slow – and I debate whether to take off on my own. I'm behind Kendra and a girl with really short hair who looks familiar from cross season. The race is 8 laps, so I figure I'll hold off another lap or two and see if I get too antsy.

It doesn't even seem like I'm racing. It's slightly faster than my jogging pace, but not by much. There are five of us in the front pack, and I know Zoe is with us by the cheering from our teammates.

They call out our splits when we finish the first mile. We're definitely on pace to hit the state qualifying time, but if we don't pick it up, this might end up being the slowest 2-mile I've raced since freshman year.

Kendra's coach yells at her and her teammate to follow through with a "negative split", meaning the second half of the race is faster than the first.

I'm only paying attention to the girl with short hair in front of me, and I don't notice that Kendra is pulling ahead until her teammate passes me. Before I can pass the girl with short hair, who isn't changing pace, Zoe passes me on the tail of the purple uniform, following Kendra and her teammate's lead.

Although I barely feel like I've been in a race up until this point, I hardly have the energy to catch up to the quicker pace. I should keep pushing forward past Zoe and move in on Kendra's heel – or pass her – but I'm suddenly feeling exhausted.

It's all I can do to hang on with Zoe.

Last race, I didn't feel tired but I couldn't go any faster. That was a new sensation. Now, it's time to go faster, and I'm exhausted. It's not necessarily a new sensation – fatigue in the middle of a race – but it's inexplicable. I've barely put forth any effort. Why does it feel like I've just run the first half of the 2-mile like it's a one-mile race?

I trudge ahead, barely paying attention to our splits as we round each lap, and ignoring Coach as he tells me to move ahead on the last turn. It's the sense of nervous energy in the group that reminds me I only have one lap to bring it home.

Kendra surges forward, and her teammate and Zoe fall behind, with me still on their tail. It's now or never.

I know I have to go with Kendra. It's what's expected of me. But my body protests. It doesn't want to feel the burn that comes with digging deeper and running faster. My legs are on cruise control, and I realize it's not so much my body that's fatigued, but my competitive spirit.

When the realization hits, it tears through me and rips me wide open. For the first time I can remember, I don't have a desire to win. I'm fine finishing right where I am.

Zoe and Kendra's teammate battle it out on the final stretch and I simply stay behind them. I watch Zoe edge out the other girl, and a small happiness for her victory washes over the deep sorrow I feel for a loss I can't explain.

I want to run off and be alone. I need to mourn whatever piece of me just disappeared. Will it ever come back?

But I don't want to act like a sore loser. Maybe that's all this is. Maybe I'm only being dramatic over a bad race. I remember Jace's words – that all athletes have bad days – but this is something different. I feel it deep in my bones. Usually after a bad race I'm ready for a comeback. I want to race again as soon as possible. Right now, I dread the next track meet.

The funny thing is that it's a lot easier to congratulate people when they beat you. I'd never realized it before. I'm able to approach Kendra without feeling like I'm rubbing it in her face that I beat her. She's a sweet girl – though I can tell she's exercising all her willpower not to ask me what happened to me on the track. I wouldn't know what to tell her anyway. I'm not sick or injured.

Coach is preoccupied watching the boys' 2-mile, and Zoe puts her warm-down on hold to cheer for Charlie. It allows me the opportunity I was hoping for to jog by myself for a few minutes. By the time Zoe catches up with me, the pain that ripped through me as I finished the race has dulled to a mild sadness. And a slight panic. Running is at the core of my identity. Without a desire to compete, who am I?

"I'm having an identity crisis," I confess to Zoe.

"How so?"

"I don't enjoy racing anymore. And even worse, I don't think I even care about winning."

Uncharacteristically, Zoe doesn't respond right away. "Do you still like running?" she asks after a moment.

"I love running," I don't hesitate to tell her.

"I think you just need a break, Pepper. Don't freak out. Just take some time off from racing. It's not such a big deal."

"I can't just quit. What will I say?" I want to get angry at her. Tell her she doesn't understand. She doesn't know what it's like. But that's not fair.

"It wouldn't be quitting. Unless you wanted to be done. Do you want that?"

"No." My tone is harsher than I intend, but the idea of never racing again cuts deep. In a way, it's comforting to know there's still some fire in me.

"Then just take the rest of track season off. Coach will let you train with us still, I'm sure, even if you don't race."

That idea is tempting, but it doesn't sit well. It feels like giving up.

"Maybe I can just do relays."

"Yeah! That's a really good idea," Zoe exclaims. And she's off talking about who might be on the 4 x 800 and DMR teams at State, and who the main competition will be.

I feel better with this new plan formed, but I'm not sure it's resolved my identity crisis. I've only put it on hold for a little longer. In the meantime, how am I supposed to reclaim my competitive spirit?

Chapter 17

When the bus returns to school, I hurry to the locker room and take a shower in record time. I'm excited to get to Wes's place and see Jace. I want to talk to him about what happened on the track today, and tell him about my new plan for the season. I'm curious what he'll think.

I've invited my friends to the party, but they're getting a bite to eat first and changing at home. Jace left his Jeep in the parking lot for me so I can drive myself to Wes's place.

I hear the party before I even turn onto Wes's street. Isn't anyone worried that the neighbors will call the cops? Although Wes's parents throw parties sometimes, so maybe the neighbors assume it's them and don't want to ruffle their feathers.

Just as Wes promised, there's a free spot in his driveway for me to park. I wander through the house, looking for Jace. A few faces are familiar from school, but some of them look older, like they might be UC students.

Twenty minutes later, I've made two rounds through the house and still no Jace. I check my phone again, but he hasn't responded to my text. Frowning, I make my way to the porch outside, for the second time, and take a soda from the cooler. It's a cool night, and there aren't many people outside.

I lean my hip against the porch railing and watch a group of guys leave the pool house. Two of them are taller than the others, and I recognize them as Brockton Public basketball players. As they draw closer, I make out their glassy eyes. They probably weren't having a book club meeting in the pool house. I glance away, toward a couple flirting on the other side of the porch.

A moment later, an arm settles around my back and squeezes my shoulder. "Pepper Jones!"

I glance up and stiffen when I recognize the owner of the arm around me.

"It's Wolfe," he says with a grin. "Remember me?"

Gulping another sip of soda to hide my reaction, I nod. I wouldn't forget a name like that. It's comical how fitting it is. Not only are his features hard – with a buzz cut that shows off a scar on his forehead – but Jace told me to stay clear of him. Even his grin has a dangerous tinge to it.

I try to duck away but he tightens his hold. "Hey Rex!" he calls to his friend, who's headed back inside. Rex turns around. "Look who I found!"

Rex checks me out as he walks back our way. "Oh yeah, you were around here awhile back when we came by." Rex points at me as he asks Wolfe, "She was the one Wilder and Wes were all, like, protective about, right?"

"Yeah, she's Wilder's girl now. Aren't you?" Wolfe asks.

I finally draw the courage to take his hand and move it off my shoulder. "Yes," I say firmly. These guys make me nervous, but I don't want them to know that.

When Jace decided to stop dealing drugs, Wolfe and Rex gave him a hard time. Jace doesn't talk about it much, but my understanding is that Jace had a connection to some dealer in Denver, and Wolfe and Rex distributed the drugs. Jace and Wes were like the middlemen. When they quit dealing, Wolfe and Rex were angry they got cut out of the whole arrangement. Apparently the dealer in Denver was a gang member and decided to move his fellow gangsters to Brockton to do the distributing.

Are they still holding a grudge against Jace? And what does that mean for me? I look around, wishing I was inside with the crowds.

My eyes sweep over to the basketball players, who are standing beside a couple of other guys who came from the pool house. The others look to be college-aged, like Rex and Wolfe. I glance toward the door inside, but the group is surrounding me, and there's no easy escape.

"Why are you all alone out here?" Wolfe asks, quickly closing the space I tried to put between us. "Did you have a fight with Jace?"

"Maybe Wesley made a move on her, Wolfe, and there's trouble in love triangle paradise," Rex says.

Gritting my teeth, I keep my mouth shut. No sense encouraging these idiots.

One of their buddies speaks up. "I bet we have something that would make her feel better."

"Yeah, a soda isn't going to help you, sweetheart," another says, commenting on the Coke gripped in my hand.

Out of the corner of my eye, I catch the basketball players say something to each other before one of them turns and hurries inside.

"Why don't we bring her to the pool house to cheer her up?" Rex asks with a laugh. He sways to the side, and his buddy holds him up when he stumbles.

I make a move to get away, but Wolfe swings an arm around my waist and pulls me to him. Tightly.

My eyes widen in shock. They are keeping me here against my will. Under Wes's roof, with Jace somewhere nearby. Of course, what better way to piss off Jace and Wes? My stomach churns, fearing how far they'll take this.

It's obvious all the guys are messed up. On what, exactly, I wouldn't know.

"Let me go," I grit out.

"You don't want to go back to the party," Wolfe coos in my ear. I flinch with disgust. "Wilder's probably with another girl. Didn't we see him going upstairs with that hot brunette chick earlier?" he asks his buddies.

My stomach rolls. They're just messing with you, I remind myself.

The next thing I know, we're moving toward the pool house. I'm fighting, but my feet keep moving in the wrong direction. Arms are around me, so to anyone watching it looks like they are supporting me. They would just think I'm another drunk girl, stumbling around. I'm not fighting harder because I can't believe this is really happening. Blood is rushing to my head and the voices around me are muffled.

The pool house is only feet away and my vision starts to blur. A small part of my brain seems to be screaming that this is not the time to lose it, that I need to be alert. But a dizziness takes over and I can't fight it. Black dots dance in front of me at the same time that Wolfe opens the pool house door. In the midst of the fear coursing through me, I think I hear loud angry voices behind me, and approaching footsteps. The arms holding me up jerk away and my knees buckle.

A moment later, I'm on the ground, puking in the grass by the pool house. The sound of grunts and thumps surround me. Glancing into the darkness, I make out several guys brawling by the edge of the pool. I blink rapidly.

Jace. He's straddled Wolfe and is pounding him. Behind them, Connor punches Rex in the jaw, and Rex stumbles backward into the pool with a giant splash. Connor spins around, looking for his next victim. Blood runs down his nose.

When I hear Rex sputtering and screaming obscenities from the pool, a burst of hysterical giggles erupts from my chest. This is ridiculous. They weren't *really* trying to force me to the pool house to take drugs or... something worse. Were they? Another round of laughter escapes me as I wipe my mouth and kneel back on my feet.

It feels like I'm watching a movie of someone else's life. This can't really be happening.

I roll onto my back, my chest rising and falling as I stare up at the stars. The chaos around me continues and I just can't stop the laughter that mixes with my heavy breathing.

Strong arms scoop me up and when I inhale the familiar woodsy scent, my laughter turns to sobs.

He doesn't say anything as he moves quickly across the lawn. I can tell when we're back inside by the warmer temperature and the loud voices. The noise quiets as Jace makes his way through the house. I bury my head in his chest, knowing we're being watched and trying to hide my tears.

Jace starts moving up the stairs and I sigh in relief that we're escaping from everyone.

"Jace, hold up!" Zoe's voice breaks through the murmuring voices, which I have no doubt are already cooking up gossip.

He pauses for a second before continuing up the stairs. "Later, Zoe," Jace says firmly. He's always been friendly to Zoe but his voice is cold, leaving no room for argument. I'm grateful for it at this moment. I just want to be alone with him.

Safe. Comforted.

Zoe, as persistent as she can be, doesn't follow us. A minute later, I breathe in deeply when I hear Jace close and lock a door, leaving the noisy party behind us.

My head lifts from his chest, his tee shirt now soaked with tears. Jace's jaw is clenched so tightly it looks painful.

He sits down on a couch, keeping me in his arms. I wouldn't let go even if he tried to disentangle us.

"You're safe now," Jace says softly. He rubs his thumb over my tear-streaked cheeks.

I'm still not sure it all really happened. Did a group of guys, high on who knows what, actually drag me with them to the pool house? Wait, we didn't make it to the pool house.

"How'd you find me?"

"Cam got me. Told me those fuckers were talking to you. When I got there..." Jace pauses and closes his eyes, shaking his head. "There were five of them. Well, four. Grayson was there, but he was about to step in."

"Cam?" My foggy brain is having trouble following him. And Jace must be pumped full of adrenaline. I can feel his heart racing and despite his gentle touch stroking my hair, his legs are clenched beneath me.

"Yeah, Cameron. He's our pitcher. And Pat Grayson. They're your grade."

"I thought they played basketball."

"Yeah, that too."

He tilts his head, probably wondering why I'm zeroing in on the least important details of what he's saying. I'm equally confused by the words coming out of my mouth. Who cares what sports they play? Maybe I'm just not ready to think about what happened.

"I think you're still in shock," Jace says quietly.

"Just kiss me," I say on a sigh.

He hesitates a moment before leaning down and taking my mouth in his. It's gentle and warm. He pulls away after a moment, and I pout.

"Pep, you taste like throw-up."

I cover my mouth with my hand, embarrassed. It's worth it for the loosening in his jaw, the restrained laughter glinting in his eyes.

"Let's get you cleaned up." Jace stands with ease, still holding me.

I take in my surroundings, recognizing it as the guest room we slept in the night of the snowstorm.

He sets me on the bathroom counter and rummages through the bathroom drawers until he finds a toothbrush. I brush my teeth while he runs a bath.

Jace helps me out of my clothes and carries me to the bath. He soaps me down, and each scrub helps erase the dirty feeling clinging to my skin.

We don't talk. Jace can tell I need silence.

Afterward, he wraps me in a towel and dresses me in sweatpants and a tee shirt twice my size.

They smell like him. My favorite woodsy spice scent.

I forgot that he started keeping some clothes at Wes's house.

Jace strips down to his boxer briefs and joins me in bed. I snuggle up to him and wrap my body in his.

As I drift off to sleep, I feel his lips on my forehead. "I'm sorry," he whispers.

I'm too tired to ask what he's apologizing for.

Chapter 18

At some point during the night, I startle awake, feeling the absence of Jace. It's not the cold that has me shivering. I'm still shaken from the night's events. I watch him unlock the door and open it a crack, light streaming in from the hallway.

He speaks quietly with someone for a few minutes before returning to bed.

I immediately wrap my arms around him, trying to get as close as possible.

"Wes got rid of those guys, Pep. They won't hurt you again. I promise."

"They didn't get a chance to hurt me, you know." I don't want there to be any confusion about that. They tried, but he stopped them. Maybe they wouldn't have done anything all that bad. I shudder. Who am I kidding? They were forcing me with them.

"They did hurt you, Pep. And not just from the bruise you'll have on your hip in the morning." I hadn't noticed it, but Wolfe's grip on me was tight.

I squirm my way up his body so I can see his face. I don't want to talk about what happened.

"Where were you when I got to the party? I couldn't find you."

Jace cringes. "I had a talk with Madeline."

"A talk?" My heart rate picks up.

Jace looks down at me disapprovingly. "I found out about the track spikes prank, Pep. I'm not happy that you didn't tell me. You shouldn't keep stuff from me."

"It didn't matter, Jace."

"It did," he says firmly. "And it felt pretty shitty hearing about it from Remy, who heard about it from Ryan."

"You boys gossip as bad as girls." But I know how that must have hurt him. He likes to think he can protect me from everything. "I'm sorry, but I'm not going to say I should have told you. Sometimes it's best to just let that kind of thing go, not give it more attention than it deserves. So, about Madeline?"

"Yeah, that's what I was talking to her about. I know she's behind those photos and messing with your shoes. It has to stop."

"So you just talked to her. That's it? I thought you already did that."

"I told her awhile back that I wasn't going to be with her again. I hadn't spoken to her since her shit against you – against us – started. If my words don't put a stop to it, though, she's going to regret ever messing with you."

"The Barbies said they'd handle it," I remind him.

"I'm not going to rely on anyone else to deal with someone hurting you, Pep. You should know that."

"Yeah, and you should know that's why I didn't tell you."

"They messed with your running. That's one of the most important things in your life."

His comment reminds me that I still haven't told him about my plan to just race relays for the rest of the track season.

I watch Jace run a hand through his hair. Even in the dark room, his features are striking. I love that I can admire his beauty up close now, after so many years of hiding my attraction.

"All this shit is because of me, Pep. The other stuff, it pisses me off. But I can handle it.

What happened tonight with Wolfe" – Jace's voice breaks and he shuts his eyes for a minute – "it kills me."

He looks me right in the eyes, letting me see his sadness.

"I should let you go," he whispers. "But I don't think I can do that."

My head snaps up. "Are you talking about breaking up with me?" Where is this coming from? He just saved me from those hooligans. He actually beat the shit out of them and carried me away.

"Those guys attacked you because they know I care about you. They wanted to hurt me by hurting you," Jace explains, laying it out for me.

"I figured that out, Jace. But they might have just been joking around. They were high. I could have gotten away or yelled or something if they really were doing something bad. Maybe they were just trying to scare me."

"They *did* scare you!" Jace sits up, pulling me with him. "You were white as a sheet when I got there. I'll never forget the look on your face!"

His breathing is rapid and I place a hand on his chest, trying to calm him.

He looks like he wants to say more. Instead, he clenches his jaw and tucks me under his chin.

"I'm so fucking sorry, Pep."

"I'm accepting your apology for threatening to break up with me." He tugs me closer. We both know that's not what he's apologizing for.

***

"Why can't you just connect those guys with whoever your dealer was? Wouldn't that get them to stop trying to hurt you, or whatever?" I refuse to say their names. But Wes and Jace know who I'm talking about.

We're lifting weights in the Jamison's private gym. Somehow, Wes managed to get people to clean up the house and kick everyone out by the time we came down for breakfast this morning.

He gave me a hug when I walked into the kitchen, but it looked like he was the one who needed it. A black bruise covered his jaw, and by the way he moved, I had a feeling there were more bruises elsewhere on his body.

I'd almost forgotten how serious the fighting had been. How did Jace get out of there without a scratch?

"Wolfe and Rex wouldn't be able to handle that much responsibility," Wes tells me. He hops down from the pull-up bar. "They party too hard."

"And they're dumb fucks," Jace adds as he settles back on the bench press, waiting for Wes to spot him.

"I don't get what that has to do with you connecting them to this gangster dude."

Wes shakes his head, smiling. "This gangster dude, Pepper, is scary. I'd rather have Wolfe and Rex's wrath than the Vegaz."

"The Vegaz?"

"That's the gang. But you didn't hear that, okay?" Wes's voice turns serious.

"Yeah, okay." I watch Jace's abs constrict as he lifts a barbell over his head.

"So if you told scary gangster dude he should give his drugs to the idiots and they messed up, the gang would take it out on you."

"Probably. It's not worth finding out."

"I didn't trust Rex and Wolfe before," Jace says as he sits up. "After last night, I really don't trust them. If Rex and Wolfe had a lot of drugs and money in their hands, they'd try to scam the Vegaz. They're that dumb."

Lifting my hand weights for the last set of bicep curls, I ask the question I'm not sure I want to hear the answer to.

"So are they going to keep attacking you until you give them what they want? It's been months and they still showed up at your party last night."

Wes and Jace share a look.

"I'd be surprised if they came back for more after last night," Jace says.

After that, I stop asking questions.

***

By the time I get home from working out with the boys, I have three missed calls from Zoe and twice as many text messages. She gets to my house in ten minutes when I ask her to meet for a run.

"I can't believe you've left me in the dark for this long! What the heck happened to you last night?" Zoe's shrill voice makes me want to cover my ears.

I steer her out of the apartment and onto the running trail, explaining a toned-down version of the night's events.

"What do you mean, 'they were giving you a hard time'? They looked like they needed a hospital by the time Jace's friends were through with them. It had to have been something bad to warrant a fight like that."

"There's a history with them. Those UC guys shouldn't have been at the party in the first place. I was just the last straw that gave them a reason to fight." I feel bad lying to Zoe – or at least not giving her the whole truth. But if I tell her what those guys were really doing, she'd completely freak out. And I just want to ignore it.

"You were crying, Pep, and people saw you lying in the grass," Zoe's voice softens.

"I just freaked out. They were scary dudes, and then I was in the middle of this crazy fight. I'm sure there are all kinds of rumors flying around, but don't believe them."

Thankfully, Zoe takes the hint and changes the subject.

"Actually, there's some other juicy gossip from last night."

"Oh yeah?"

"You know Brad Simmons? Captain of the lacrosse team? Dorothy was hooking up with him at the party and she didn't make it to a bathroom in time. Stunk up her jeans and everything."

I burst into laughter. "You can't be serious."

"Yup. The Barbies put copious amounts of laxatives in her drink. She was in the bathroom most of the night. Probably wanted to get home but was too drunk to drive, and I bet no one wanted her stinky butt in their car to give her a ride."

My laughter dies down a little when I think about how awful the night must have been for her. Man, the Barbies are brutal.

"I feel pretty bad," I admit. "That's a really mean way to get back at her."

"Yeah, it's not nice. But hey, she tried to break up two couples. And you and Jace are awesome together. That was pretty cruel. She could've ruined your relationship and friendship. Who knows what else she had planned besides the shoe-stealing stuff?"

"Yeah, Dorothy's not exactly a nice girl herself. Think she learned her lesson?"

"Doubt it."

Jace is even more attentive than usual the next few days. He texts me throughout the day and meets me between all my classes. He brings me treats – donuts, brownies, muffins – each day. It helps make up for all the curious stares from other students.

I know that Jace was right, in a way, that what happened on Saturday night was a result of us being together. And it could have been a whole lot worse. But I don't blame him. Yeah, he was an idiot to deal drugs – especially with so many shady characters – but he stopped. And he never thought it would come back to hurt me.

As for jealous girls like Madeline coming after me... well, Jace can't exactly help being drop-dead gorgeous. Maybe he didn't need to sleep with so many girls, but he never made them any promises.

But Jace still acts like he's done me wrong. Like he was the one who hurt me. He's not as confident around me. Despite his attentiveness, he's acting almost ashamed of himself, as though he doesn't deserve to let his guard down and be himself with me.

When I finally get around to telling him, Jace likes my idea to just race relays the rest of the season. He says it's bumming him out that I don't get excited about racing anymore, and maybe taking a break from individual events is what I need. It gives me enough confidence in my decision to bring it up to Coach.

"If that's what you need right now, Pepper, then I'll support you," Coach tells me. "There's something else I need to talk to you about though."

"Something else?" I can't imagine what it would be.

"Have you entered your info on the NCAA website?"

"What do you mean?"

Coach shakes his head with a look of disbelief. "So that college coaches can contact you. To recruit you," he adds, when I give him a blank look.

"Oh, right." I laugh at myself. I hadn't even thought about college recruitment. "Is now when they start recruiting? I guess I thought I had until senior year to think about it."

"Coaches have been calling me trying to get through to you over the past month. I can't give them your info without your permission. It didn't seem the best time to bring it up with you, but you need to start thinking about it. You're going to have a lot of choices."

I sigh. "Maybe. But I already know I want to go to UC, so there's not a lot to think about."

Coach puts his hand on my shoulder. It's something he always does when he wants me to pay attention. "You should at least take advantage of the recruiting trips to visit other colleges, Pepper. See other parts of the country and get a feel for what other teams and colleges could offer you. Then you'll be able to make an informed decision."

I shrug. "Maybe," I say again. I can agree with getting free trips to visit other schools. It might not be entirely morally sound, if I know I won't go to their school, but they can always advertise that the national champion showed interest in their program. So it's a win-win. "We'll see."

The following Saturday is our only home meet. We don't have the best track in the area, so it's just a low-key meet with three other schools. My only race is the 4 x 800. Jace's game is earlier in the day and he's able to come by to watch.

He's with Remy, and the two of them attract a lot of attention sitting in the stands. It's not often the most popular guys in school come to watch our meets. I catch the girls from the other schools ogling Jace and I grin. I'm lucky that he's all mine.

His presence makes me want to race well. But it doesn't make me anxious and nervous the way expectations from others do. I wish he could come to all my meets.

And I do race well. Nothing spectacular – I've never been awesome at the 800 distance – but not a disaster either. I'm able to move the relay from second to first, and it always feels good to win.

"Hey guys, how was your game?" I jog over to Remy and Jace before starting my cool down.

"Thanks to your boy here, we won 8-6. He hit a triple in the last inning," Remy tells me.

Jace tugs me into his chest and kisses my forehead. "Nice race, Pep. You killed it."

"Thanks." I close my eyes and smile at the feel of his lips on my forehead, his strong arms around my waist.

"You should head over to the tennis courts when you finish up here."

I lean back and raise my eyebrows. We don't usually watch tennis matches.

Jace gives me a mischievous smirk. "Kayla and the girls told us to watch. They're playing Lincoln Academy."

A shiver runs through me. Madeline is the captain of Lincoln's tennis team. Did the Barbies pull another laxative prank? I'm not sure I want to witness that.

Still, curiosity compels me to show up thirty minutes later with Zoe, Claire, Charlie, Rollie, and Ryan. When I told Zoe the Barbies asked us to watch the game, she spread the word. There's a hill overlooking the courts and it's scattered with spectators. Jace and Remy have prime seating at the top and center of the hill, and they clear space for us when they see us coming.

I'm surprised to see Wesley sitting next to them.

"Sorry I missed your race, Pep," he says, standing up to greet me with a hug. "Just got here."

As far as I know, Wes doesn't normally watch girls' tennis either. He must be here for the same reason we are. In fact, looking around, the crowd seems unusually large.

"Madeline and Emma are playing Lisa and Andrea in doubles," Jace tells me as he settles me between his legs.

Well, that match-up alone will be entertaining.

The girls have just finished warming up, and Lincoln serves first. The teams are fairly evenly matched and it's point for point. But the close match and rivalry between the schools can't be why we're here.

It's fifteen minutes into the match when I start to notice Madeline's game changing. She doesn't get to the balls quickly enough, and when she does, she hits them out of bounds. Like, *way* out of bounds.

I glance around, trying to determine if anyone else notices the difference. Is it all in my head because I'm looking for it? I glance back at Jace, who leans forward and whispers, "Just keep watching, Pep."

I turn my eyes back to the court, and watch Madeline walk slowly to the line to take her serve. Emma is crouched in position by the net, but keeps glancing back nervously, clearly wondering what is taking Madeline so long.

Madeline rolls the tennis ball around in her palm, staring at it with concentration. It must be minutes later when she sighs, finally tossing it in the air and swinging her racket. She completely misses the ball and almost falls on her face after swinging her racket blindly in the air. I hear gasps from those watching around me.

The expression on her face is one I've never witnessed. She's lost her cool. And Madeline Brescoll actually looks embarrassed. That alone is satisfying. But it gets worse. A lot worse.

Madeline pulls a ball from a hidden pocket in her tennis skirt and takes a second serve. She successfully connects her racket with the ball, but it hits Emma in the bum. Emma squeals and grabs her bottom while jumping in the air. The crowd roars. I have a hard time controlling my own laughter.

There's something satisfying about seeing such girls who are usually so put-together and cool acting ridiculous.

Madeline keeps attempting to serve, usually whiffing, but occasionally connecting with the ball only to hit it backwards or out of bounds. The funniest thing is that she seems oblivious to her horrendous playing.

"What did they do to her?" I ask Jace.

"I have my suspicions." The corners of his mouth turn up. "But let's wait and see."

When Brockton Public serves, Madeline's play continues to deteriorate. At one point, she runs right into the net in an attempt to get to a ball. She flies over the net, half her body on Lincoln's side of the court, and half on Brockton Public's.

Emma helps her off, and pulls her aside, talking animatedly. They've now attracted attention from players on the other courts, who have paused in their own matches to watch the spectacle.

Suddenly, Madeline erupts in ear-splitting laughter. She falls to her knees, the sound so screechy it pierces the air. Emma tugs her up to her feet, and places her hands on her hips, apparently scolding Madeline, but we can't hear her words.

They attempt to resume the game, Madeline's play becoming increasingly erratic and pitiful. When she hits herself in the head with her own racket and twirls around looking for the ball, their coach intervenes. After a brief discussion with Madeline and Emma, he announces a forfeit.

"*Now* are you going to tell me what you think they did to her?"

Jace speaks quietly in my ear, aware that others are probably trying to listen in. "My theory? They somehow got pot into something she ate."

They drugged her. Like they drugged Dorothy. If this is part of their wicked game, what will be Madeline's next move? And will *I* be the victim? The blood drains from my face.

"Hey, hey," Jace soothes, stroking my cheek. "No one's going to mess with you anymore. That's what the point of all of this was."

I want to believe him, but I don't.

Chapter 19

Jace was right about the pot. Kayla, Lisa and Andrea baked muffins and granola bars with pot butter. They wanted to make sure Madeline would eat at least one of the baked goods, and she ended up eating both. One of Madeline's teammates, whom Madeline apparently pissed off when she slept with the girl's boyfriend, helped the Barbies out. I could see that plan going *very* badly wrong – with the whole team accidentally eating the baked goods – but the teammate orchestrated it flawlessly.

We learn all this over pizza at Lou's. Kayla is especially proud of herself, and by the time we're ready to leave, she is plastered. Her cousin waited on our table again, and she convinced him to serve her whisky shots in celebration of their successful prank.

I'm not sure how I feel about all of it. I know it wasn't my idea. But I laughed along with everyone else, and I'm hanging out with them while they celebrate. Does that make me just as mean?

In the parking lot outside Lou's, Jace's friends decide to meet up at Ben's house.

"Pepper and I are heading to my place," Jace tells them.

The guys give him a hard time about it, but he says we have plans to hang out with Wesley. It's true – Wes didn't want to come to Lou's with us, claiming the tiff between the Lincoln and Public girls puts him in an awkward position. He doesn't want to be seen as taking sides.

"I side with you and my brother," he'd told me in a low voice after the tennis match.

Wes is already at the Wilders' house by the time we get there. He sits with Jim in the kitchen, drinking a beer. Jim doesn't try to pretend that his sons don't drink. It still surprises me sometimes to see the two of them together like father and son. But once they started hanging out again, their relationship came easily.

It's rare that I hang out with the three of them at the same time, and I feel a bit like an intruder. Even though Jace made his friends believe he ditched them for alone time with me, it was really for family time. No one else knows that Wes is his half-brother.

I stop wondering whether I should leave so they can have father-son-brother bonding time once we settle in for a game of poker. Jace holds my feet in his lap, and the guys include me just like I'm part of the family. It feels good.

Warm and fuzzy. Gran would fit right in too. Maybe next time I'll invite her.

They're giving me a hard time about how I pretend to be clueless but I keep winning when we hear several phones beep with text message alerts. Wes, Jace and I look at each other in anticipation.

There's no way she retaliated that fast.

"Well, is anyone going to check their messages?" Jim asks.

None of us move, and we continue to glance at each other.

"What's going on, guys?" he asks.

"We'll have to check it eventually," Wes says. He's right.

I remove mine from my sweatshirt pocket and see it's a video. Oh joy.

"I'll look first." The guys watch me as I click on it.

It's dark and there's a rustling sound as the picture comes into focus. An object is moving back and forth. No, up and down. The video zooms in, and I see it's a head, with long dark wavy hair. Her head is between two legs.

Oh no.

But I can't stop watching as the sound of heavy breathing comes through my phone. The video moves up the legs to show the body lying on a bed, his arms behind his head. And then he lifts his head up to say something to the girl. The chiseled cheekbones and messy black hair are unmistakable.

Jace grabs the phone out of my hand, takes one look at it, and throws it across the room. It hits the refrigerator, but doesn't shatter.

My heart clenches. Is the video from last Saturday night? When he said he was talking to her, is this what he really meant?

He's on his feet, looking like he's going to pick up his chair and throw that across the room too. Jim stands up and puts his hand on Jace's shoulder.

"Jace," he says sternly. That's all he says. Jim has no idea what's going on, what the video was, but his presence might be the only thing preventing me from screaming and Jace from destroying the house.

I can feel Wes watching me. And when Jace's gaze finally turns to me, he rushes to my side, crouching in front of me. I haven't shed any tears yet. In fact, my face feels numb. It's my chest that feels like it's going to explode with pain.

"I'm sorry you had to see that, Pep." He takes my hands and leans forward to cradle my head in his chest. I stiffen. I don't mean to, my body just can't be that close to him right now.

His face contorts in anguish. Is there remorse there too?

"You know it's from before us, right?" he asks slowly. "I would never do that to you, Pep. You believe me, don't you?"

I gulp down a lump in my throat. Oh, I want to believe him. But all I see is Madeline's head moving over him, his abs clenching as he sits up to say something to her, the look of enjoyment on his face when he relaxes back on the bed.

Jim and Wes are watching us, and I think I see sadness, or pity, in their eyes. For me, or for Jace?

"I just need to be alone for a minute," I choke the words out.

Jace shakes his head, panic overcoming his beautiful features.

"Pep," he pleads, trying to pull me to him as I stand up on shaky legs.

I want that video to be from a long time ago. I want the images erased from my brain. And I want to go back to ten minutes earlier, before it was sent. But right now, all I know is I can't be here. My heart is hammering so hard that it's not leaving much room for me to think.

"Just give me tonight to process this," I say, searching his face, hoping he'll understand that I don't know what to feel right now. If he broke my trust, I should feel anger, and if it's someone using his past to hurt us, I should be fighting for him. But there's just confusion wrapped around the pounding in my chest.

Wes is behind me, placing a hand on the small of my back. "I'll walk her home, Jace."

Jace shoves Wes's arm off me and pulls me to him, giving me no choice but to bury my head in his chest. "Please, Pep, don't do this." His breath is in my ear, and I wish I could just crumble, let him comfort me, and forget this happened.

"I'm not doing anything, Jace." I pull away and walk shakily down the stairs to the front door without looking at anyone. The cool night air hits me, and as I make my way to the sidewalk, the tears start to flow. They aren't hard sobs, just gentle tears that run slowly down my cheeks.

I turn around at the sound of footsteps, expecting Jace. But it's Wes there with my bag, which I hadn't even realized I'd left behind.

He hands it to me and we continue walking in silence.

"I haven't looked at the video," he says when we get to my apartment building. "All I can tell you is I'd be shocked if he cheated on you. He's wanted you for a long time, Pepper, and now that he has you, I don't think he'd do anything intentionally to mess it up."

Wes's words linger in my head as I make my way up the stairs to my apartment and into my bedroom. His faith in Jace means something, but I don't miss that Wes left some room for doubt. He said he'd be *shocked* if Jace cheated on me, not that he knows Jace didn't. He doesn't *think* Jace would do anything *intentionally*, but he doesn't know it either.

But I've seen Madeline with guys before. She literally turns heads. And when she turns on the charm, guys melt at her feet. Maybe even do things they don't intend to.

***

I don't sleep much that night, and it's still dark out when I wake up to my phone ringing.

It's Jace. I let it go to voicemail and check the time. 5:48 in the morning. He gave me some time to process it, but I need more.

I've tossed and turned in my bed, my thoughts going back and forth and around in circles.

I remember Wolfe's words at Wes's party. He saw them go upstairs together. Jace admitted he talked to Madeline, but he seemed to have been gone for a long time based on how long I was looking for him.

What about when he said he was sorry? Maybe he was talking about cheating on me. No, he was talking about Wolfe and Rex.

But I've never done to Jace what Madeline was doing. Only because he insists on taking it slow. Is he being patient with me because he's sleeping with other girls? Ugh!

I rip my sheets off and sit up in bed. My head is its very own ping pong match. The thoughts are driving me insane.

And the worst part is, I feel absolutely terrible for doubting him at all. He trusted my word about the photos with Ryan. Shouldn't I do the same for him?

This feels different, though.

Dave watches me with concern from the foot of my bed. He wiggles up next to me and nudges my thigh with his nose.

I sigh heavily and rub his ears.

"Let's go for a run," I tell him.

I make the mistake of glancing at my phone again before leaving. It has been on silent all night and I see there are missed calls and texts from Zoe. That means the video's gone viral.

As my feet hit the pavement, it dawns on me that the video humiliates Madeline too. Would she really put a pornographic video out of herself just to break up me and Jace? Besides, she must suspect that the retaliation was initiated by the Barbies, not me. Who would spy on them like that and record it?

I inhale the fresh morning air and try to let the sound of the creek and chirping birds clear my head.

The love I feel for Jace is so intense that it absolutely crushes me to think he could betray me. He's hasn't given me any reason to distrust him. Yet, if I believe him on this, it means I'm surrendering everything to this boy. I'll be more vulnerable than ever before. In the past, hearing about him with other girls pierced me, and left me with a queasy stomach. But I've always kept a shield up, however flimsy, to protect myself from my own feelings for him. Without it, he has the power to break me. If I take his word about the video and later find out he's been unfaithful, I'm not sure I'll ever be the same again. My body shudders.

I'm still letting my head swarm with possibilities as I jog along the familiar path. He was angry last night, but didn't look confused or surprised by the video. Was he so upset because he knew he made a mistake, or because the video hurt me?

I'm still not feeling any better by the time I turn around on the dirt trail to head home. Dave senses my mood and his gait is subdued. He refrains from chasing a squirrel, and instead glances at me cautiously. I know, buddy, I'm a hot mess.

We take a turn into the woods and I come to a halt before colliding with a familiar chest. Jace is breathing heavily, his hair even messier than usual, and his eyes are dry and red. We're nearly two miles from home, and he never goes for runs unless he's forced to for football or baseball training.

My immediate reaction is to comfort him, and I step forward to reach for him, before the image of him lying on a bed, a girl between his legs, pops unwillingly into my head. His jaw clenches as he watches me retract my hand.

Dave's head swings back and forth. He's unaccustomed to the tension between us.

"I'm sorry." The apology spills from my mouth, and I'm not sure where it comes from.

"*You're* sorry?"

"For not believing you. You believed me, and I've doubted you."

"So you believe me now?" He looks like he wants to close the space between us, but holds himself back.

My eyes drift down to my feet. Why am I so ashamed of myself for being distrustful? He's been with so many girls over the years; it's only right that I question his newfound monogamy. Right?

"I *want* to believe you, Jace." I can't meet his eyes.

He takes a step forward and tilts my chin up with his finger, forcing me to look at him.

"So just believe me, then." It's a cross between a command and a plea.

I nod. With years of friendship between us, I should at least be able to give him the benefit of the doubt. If I keep pushing him away while I figure it out, who knows how much harder it will be to fix things? Or if our relationship would even *be* fixable. It's better if we work through this together.

We jog back along the trail side by side, Dave forging the way. When we get to Shadow Lane, we slow to a walk. Jace takes my hand and kisses me on the cheek. The sunrise is in front of us, and in this moment, just for these brief minutes at least, I'm content.

***

I hadn't even considered the consequences at school if Jace and I hadn't made a united front. Everyone is talking about the video. Because we're still together, the consensus is that it was another prank – like the photos of me and Ryan. But there are some who believe Jace gets around and that I allow it. A part of me still wonders if those rumors are true. Will I ever stop wondering?

The hotter topic of discussion is less about our relationship and more about who sent the video. No one seems to know.

When Wesley confronted Madeline about the video, she acted outraged that it had gone viral. But she wouldn't say when it was taken.

Even if she didn't send it, she's smart enough to use it to advance her ploy.

Whoever sent the video, if their intention was to put a rift between Jace and me, they succeeded. I haven't decided if I trust him yet, and he knows it.

Unlike last week, when he spent all his free time with me, he seems to be avoiding me now. We can't be fake together, and it's painful knowing there's a lack of trust between us. It's easier not to spend time together.

"What do you guys think?" I finally ask Jenny, Claire and Zoe when we're on an easy run. It's Friday, the day before the District Championships, but the last thing on my mind is racing.

I've been reluctant to ask for their opinions, fearing their answers. They've sensed this, and haven't brought up the video with me yet.

"I don't think he did it while you were together, Pepper," Zoe says. "I've started to get over how gorgeous and intimidating he is over the last few months, and now I can really see how he feels for you. I've only missed it over the years because it's hard to focus on anything but his hotness when he's around."

"It's not so much that I doubt how he feels. It's that I doubt his ability to be with just me. I've made an effort to ignore his past before, but now... I just wonder if I've been naïve thinking he could go from so many girls to me." Especially since we don't have sex, I think. But that's our private business.

"I guess you should know that Madeline has been implying that the video was from last Saturday night, and hinting it's not the first time that's happened while he's been with you," Claire says quietly. She doesn't listen much to gossip, so this information must be pretty well-known. I know she's only trying to protect me from further humiliation by telling me.

"It's a smart tactic on her part," Jenny comments. "By being subtle about it and not so in-your-face, she makes it more believable. But I don't believe her."

"So, don't get mad," Zoe begins, "but we were talking about it at lunch yesterday. Omar was at the party and he saw Jace and Madeline go upstairs together. But he said they were up there for, like, two minutes, and it totally didn't seem like anything happened. She actually looked pissed when she came back downstairs. I didn't tell you earlier because you didn't want to talk about it," Zoe adds quickly.

"He told me he talked to her, so I already knew they were together that night," I explain. "I just wish I could erase the video from my head."

I'm not cut out for the popular social circles. I don't know how to play their game. How do I know what's real and what isn't? On top of it all, I'm afraid to go to any more parties after what happened with Rex and Wolfe. What if they show up again?

Our relationship was finally starting to meld into the rest of our lives. I'd found my place amongst his friends and social life, and Jace was getting to know my friends, who were slowly becoming less intimidated by him. It was going so well, and it seems like overnight I'm questioning everything.

Chapter 20

By Saturday, I haven't see Jace since Thursday morning, when he gave me a ride to school.

I can hardly believe it's the District Championships already. The track season has flown by. After this one, there's only State.

The 4 x 800 is nothing special. It's not a race I ever get particularly excited about, and there have never been high expectations on me to rock the half-mile leg of that race. We place third, a solid finish.

The DMR is the last race of the day and I find myself actually looking forward to it. In the midst of everything that's happened in the last couple of weeks, my anxiety about racing feels insignificant. I was nearly forced against my will into a pool house by a group of college guys, and I watched a video of a girl who hates me give a blowjob to my boyfriend. Why should I even care that other people have high expectations of me on the track? I'm tougher than that. Competition has always been my thing, and I won't let my own success cripple me. It's a revelation that lifts a heavy weight from my shoulders.

Because the DMR has a different distance for each leg of the relay, it's an especially fun race to watch. Plus, it's the last race of the meet, and everyone else is done with their events. Brockton Public and Everfield High have been neck and neck throughout the day's competition. The announcer has kept us apprised of the point tally, and it's come down to the last event.

For the first time this season, the pressure to race well feels good. I've been so consumed with emotional turmoil, it's refreshing to focus on something so pure and simple. Just run fast and win the race.

Zoe races the first leg – 1200 meters, or 3 laps around the track. She raced the 2-mile earlier in the day, but she runs a strong race, coming in with the top group of four other runners. We're not concerned with the other teams. It's Everfield High we need to beat.

A girl that everyone calls Zippy (her real name is Liz, but even the teachers call her Zippy) races the 400. Her main event is the 400 hurdles but she's also the fastest person on our team in the 400. Zippy moves us in front of the lead pack, but Everfield is right on her heels.

I bounce up and down, cheering words of encouragement to Jenny. She's proven herself in the 800, and has the speed to keep us in the running. Unfortunately, the 800 leg for Everfield placed second in the individual 800 race earlier today, and Jenny can't keep up. She comes around the last corner 10 meters behind Everfield.

I like being the underdog when I anchor a relay. But I've got my work cut out for me. I'm running the longest leg – the mile, 4 laps around the track. The Everfield anchor won the individual mile, and is ranked first in the event in the state. She regularly clocks under 5-minute miles, and I've never broken 5 minutes myself.

As soon as Jenny hands me the baton, I don't hold back. My legs reject my usual conservative racing approach. As the anchor, I'll either catch Everfield and Brockton Public wins Districts, or I won't. Might as well get to her as fast as I can and see what happens. My body feels alive for the first time this season, and I'm going with it.

The roar of the crowd fuels my energy, and I easily lap two other runners as I make my way closer to the purple uniform. It takes me two laps to reach her.

She's not a runner I recognize. Coach told me she plays soccer in the fall instead of running cross country. Apparently she's known to give a hell of a sprint at the finish, and I need to be in a good position to hold my own. I'm feeling strong, like I can pick up the pace. Should I move ahead in anticipation of her sprint finish? If I stay with her she might outkick me. But I rarely move into the lead unless I'm sure I've got the reserve to keep up the pace; I'm hesitant to test my limits.

"Stop hesitating, Pepper. Pass her!" Coach yells. He knows me too well.

There's still a lap and a half left and she's holding a very fast pace already. I know if I pick up the pace I risk burning up. But my body is eager to prove itself and I dig deep for the courage to take the lead. I want to leave everything else going on in my life behind. It feels like if I can face down my fears on the track, I can take on everything else off the track too.

As soon as I stop holding back, a new round of energy takes hold of me and I simply zoom forward, leaving all my insecurities about proving myself on the track or burning out at the end of the race behind me.

"Pepper Jones just took this race to a new level! Katerina Davis is trying to hold on to Pepper's pace, but boy has she dropped the hammer! Look at her go!" The announcer is a goofy guy, but his words ignite my competitive spirit and I'm determined to leave this Katerina Davis in the dust. The bell rings loudly as we pass through the finish for the last lap.

My teammates scream encouragements and it propels me forward. I can't forget that Katerina will sprint the last 100 meters and if I don't get ahead now, she might pass me. I have a good kick, but I'm a distance runner first and foremost, and the top miler in the state is bound to have a faster sprint than me.

When I round the last curve into the final stretch, the loudspeaker announces that "it looks like Brockton Public will take home the team trophy this year!" Hearing those words, it's tempting to succumb to the fatigue that is now taking over, but I won't assume that my lead is enough. Why win by a little when I can win by a lot?

I race to the finish like she's right next to me, even though the crowd tells me I've already claimed first. It simply feels good to push my body, and feel that familiar fire inside that tells me I've given it my all. I rip through the finish line, and I'm greeted with high fives by my teammates.

What a rush.

My split is well under five minutes. I've slammed my personal record in the mile.

After a cool down, I make my way over to Gran. She's sitting in the stands with two other women, and when they turn to face me I recognize Annie and Helen. I can't hide my surprise at seeing them here.

"We wanted to watch one of your meets, Pepper!" Annie exclaims. "I hope you don't mind."

"No, that's cool. Thanks for coming." They congratulate me on the relay, and I smile politely at their praise.

Gran examines me for a moment before announcing that she invited Helen and Annie for dinner. "Jace too, but he told me he's got an overnight baseball game or something."

Annie laughs. "The game isn't overnight, Bunny. He just has games today and tomorrow so the team is staying in a motel down there."

Frowning, I realize I didn't even know he'd be out of town. The games must have been rescheduled at the last minute or something because they aren't usually scheduled for Sunday. He never said goodbye. We've both been closed off this week. I can't tell if he's feeling upset with me for hesitating in trusting him, or guilty from cheating on me.

"You talked to him?" I ask Gran.

"This morning. They were on the road."

Helen already has dinner plans, so we offer Annie a ride to our place, since they came together.

I text Jace on the way, asking how the games went, and telling him I miss him. I do. It's weird hanging out with Annie without him. And I can't wait to tell him about my race today.

It's only been four months since Annie moved back, but she's changed significantly. She teases Gran about her soap opera addiction and asks for some easy dinner recipes so that she can start cooking.

"I'm applying to a job at the public library," she tells us. "I want to have more regular hours. The people in my Narcotics Anonymous group all say that a stable routine is really helpful."

She's taking initiative, and she seems happy.

For someone I initially took as passive and lacking a backbone, she surprises me by bringing up Jace when I drive her home.

"He told me what's been going on. How are you feeling about it?"

It's the first time we've been alone together, and she cuts right to the chase.

"Uh… he talked to you about that?" I highly doubt he told her many details. It's not like him to open up at all. I'm certainly not prepared to get personal with Annie, even if I have begun to warm up to her.

"He told me about the video, and that you won't trust him."

"He said that?" It's hard to imagine Jace having a heart-to-heart with his mom about our relationship.

"I could tell he was torn up about something, so I asked him what it was. He's hurting bad, Pepper."

My eyes narrow as I turn onto the road to Helen's condo. Is she trying to guilt trip me?

"I told him that I believed him. I'm trying." My voice has an edge to it and I wish I didn't sound so defensive. I certainly can't tell Annie that it's possible her son really did cheat on me.

As I pull up outside the condo, Annie unbuckles her seatbelt and puts her hand on my arm.

"I'm not going to tell you what to do, Pepper. But I've gotten to know you well enough these past months to see that you're a thinker. You think through everything before you act. It's a great quality. But this isn't the kind of thing that you can think through and come up with the right answer. It's more a heart thing."

"Are you trying to tell me I should listen to my heart?" I smile and raise my eyebrows. She laughs, breaking the serious moment.

"I know, it's incredibly cheesy. But I want to try being a mom to both of you, and that's the best advice I have. Try not to think so hard and listen to your heart on this one."

She winks and hops out of the car.

My heart knows exactly how it feels, and it practically bursts as I drive home, as though it's relieved I'm finally listening to it.

Chapter 21

I try calling Jace as soon as I get home but it goes straight to voicemail. He probably forgot his charger. Normally he'd at least check in from someone else's phone, but I don't hear from him. I'm not worried. We've been having this weird standoff, and Jace is never one to pretend things are okay when they aren't. I can't halfway commit to trusting him anymore. It's all or nothing.

By Sunday afternoon I'm too impatient to wait any longer. I walk over to his house. No one's home, but I have a key to let myself in. I head downstairs and peek in his room. A hoodie lies on the floor and I pick it up. It smells like Jace. It's only been three days since I've seen him, but I miss him.

I slip on his hoodie and settle onto the couch to work on a puzzle we started a couple of weeks ago.

The doorbell rings thirty minutes later, and I wonder if I should answer it. Maybe it's Sheila here to meet Jim? But when I open the door, Madeline Brescoll stands before me.

My heart drops to my stomach.

"Oh, Pepper," she says dismissively. "I didn't expect to see you here." She gives me a fake smile.

"Same," I reply through gritted teeth.

"I'm here to see Jace," she tells me.

"I figured." I'm not used to being snarky but she brings out the worst in me. It's hard to be nice to the girl who's trying to get in the middle of my relationship with Jace. "He's not here," I tell her.

"Oh? That's funny, he asked me to meet him."

"Did he?" I straighten my shoulders.

We stare at each other for a moment.

"Maybe I should come back later," she offers smoothly.

"What time did he ask you to come over?" I ask her before she turns to leave.

"Around now. The team bus just got back to the high school, and he's coming straight home."

I know how her scheming works now, and I'm not going to leave it to Jace to explain why Madeline showed up at his door. I can either let her push me around, or push her myself. If I'm putting my trust in the wrong person, I risk being humiliated. But that's a small price to pay when the alternative could be losing Jace.

"Oh yeah? Did he call to tell you that?"

She falters for a split second before answering, but I catch her hesitation. "He texted me. Why do you ask?"

"Can I see your phone?"

"I deleted the text, Pepper. Obviously, he hasn't broken up with you yet and I'm supposed to keep our hook-ups a secret. But you're too naïve to know how these things work," she says snidely, as though sophistication in cheating is an admirable quality.

"A secret? Is that what you call a video that goes viral? Or your vague answers to everyone about when that video was taken?"

She brushes her hair out of her face. "You must be even stupider than I thought if you think I sent that video out. And I was just trying to respect Jace's wishes by not telling everyone he's been cheating on you with me. But I didn't want to be a liar either. So it put me in a difficult position."

Man, this girl has an answer to everything. But my gut (or maybe it's my heart?) tells me she's lying. And she's a *very* good liar. I have to be strong. My faith in Jace has to be stronger.

"Why don't you just let me see your phone so I can see who told you the team was back?"

"No. You're paranoid. Can't you just see what's right in front of you? He got tired of you and came back to me. Just like I warned you he would!" Madeline's voice is shrill, and she's losing her calm façade fast.

I cross my arms and glare at her. I won't be one of her victims any more.

She spins around and walks toward her car. Before she reaches it, Jace's Jeep turns onto Shadow Lane. She pauses mid-stride.

He pulls into the driveway and hops out. He walks straight toward me, ignoring Madeline completely. Before I can utter a word, I'm in his arms in a tight embrace, and his lips descend on mine. My head is spinning when he releases me. He searches my eyes for a moment before finally turning to Madeline.

"Why are you here?" he asks coldly.

"You know why I'm here, Jace," she says sweetly. "You told me to meet you. It's probably time to stop pretending with Pepper. I know you feel guilty since you've been friends a long time, but leading her on like this is becoming sort of cruel, don't you think?"

She is just too much. Didn't she just witness that display of affection?

Jace shakes his head in disbelief and turns to me with a questioning look.

"I was waiting for you to get home and she showed up. She said you texted her to tell her to meet you, but she wouldn't show me the message," I quickly summarize the conversation.

"Let's see your phone," Jace demands.

"Stop being an asshole, Jace," she responds.

Jace stalks over to her. "Stop playing games, Madeline, and I will."

"This is ridiculous!" she stammers.

"It got ridiculous when you took it this far to try to get my girlfriend to break up with me. When I wouldn't break up with her over those photos, you decided to send that video. I don't know why you had that video in the first place, but your game is starting to get pretty sick."

Madeline takes a step back. "I didn't send the video."

Jace puts his hand out. "Just hand over your phone." His tone leaves no room for argument and after a long minute, she reaches into her purse and places it in his hand.

He touches the screen a few times before pulling up what he's looking for. Jace's jaw clenches. "That little shit," he murmurs.

He walks back to me with the phone and hands it to me. "It was Ethan Lawrence."

I look at the screen. Sure enough, there's a message from Ethan telling Madeline that the team just got to the school parking lot, and Jace is going straight home.

"Who's Ethan?" I ask. Not that it matters.

"The only freshman on the team. I'll give him a break this time. He probably didn't know he was playing with fire."

Jace tosses her the phone and she fumbles it, dropping it on the sidewalk.

He takes my hand and tugs me inside, shutting the door on Madeline Brescoll and leaving her behind us.

I wrap my arms around Jace's neck. "I missed you," I tell him. And I don't just mean over this weekend, but throughout the week. Ever since the video was sent.

"I know." Jace's face lights up. "You're like this little fireball of confidence. It's a sexy look on you."

I lean my head back and press my hips further into his. "I had some revelations this weekend."

"I noticed." Jace's eyes darken and his hands move down lower on my back, resting at the top of my jeans.

"Mmmhmm. I don't just have a newfound confidence in dealing with Mad-Evil Brescoll, but I also rediscovered my competitive spirit."

He lifts me up with a grin and I wrap my legs around his waist as he carries me down the stairs to his bedroom.

He asks me about my race while peeling off my jeans. I quickly become too distracted to focus.

"It sounds like you deserve a leg massage after a race like that. Maybe a butt massage too." He hooks his fingers in my panties and tugs them down to join the pile with my jeans. Then he kisses my hip and gets to know each and every one of my muscles from the waist down.

***

Later that night, Jace makes grilled cheese sandwiches while I watch him from the kitchen counter.

"Did you have any idea that Mad-Evil was so crazy?" I ask him.

Jace takes my cheeks in his hands and brushes his nose with mine. "Mad-Evil, huh? Cute." He slices my sandwich in half and hands it to me. "If I'd known she was so obsessed, I would have handled it differently. And I definitely wouldn't have touched her in the first place."

"Do you think she sent that video?" I ask before taking a bite.

He leans against the counter next to me and crosses his arms.

"I don't know."

We don't talk about how it took me a week to decide I believed him, or what made me come around. Maybe the cheesy advice from Annie did the trick, I don't know. I do know that I really didn't want to face a world without Jace. And if he cheated on me, I'm not sure I'd be able to forgive him.

"What happened to the kitchen stools that used to be here?" I wonder.

"We're getting new ones."

"You could have kept the old ones until then. I liked those chairs. You could spin around on them."

"I kind of destroyed them in a moment of frustration," Jace admits.

I raise my eyebrows in a question.

He blows out a sigh and looks at the ceiling. "I was pretty angry when you left the house." He turns to face me. "Not at you. I get why you did. But then when Wes went running after you... it took a lot of self-control not to stop you. I guess I went a little crazy."

I imagine Jim witnessing Jace's outburst. "Your dad didn't stop you."

"He tried for a minute and then I guess he figured I needed to let it all out. Better the furniture than a person, right?"

The doorbell rings, and I jump at the noise. "If that's Mad-Evil," I start to say. But we hear Wes's voice when he opens the door.

"Hey, lovebirds! You aren't naked, are you?" he calls out.

"We're in the kitchen," Jace responds. "Clothed!" he adds.

I roll my eyes.

"I've got some news," he announces before hopping up on the other end of the counter. "Still haven't replaced the stools?" he asks Jace.

Jace smacks him lightly on the back of the head. "Fuck off."

"What's your news?" I bring them back on track.

"Wolfe, the sick fuck, sent the video," he says coolly, like he didn't just deliver a pretty major revelation. "Can you make me a grilled cheese too?"

"How'd you figure that out?" Jace asks as he slices up more cheddar cheese.

"I thought of who your enemies were, and he's the only one screwed up enough to do something like that." He pauses before adding, "Though I guess some girls out there might be obsessed enough." He shakes his head at that disturbing thought. "Anyway, took a bunch of guys with me to Wolfe's place last night. He was there. High with some chick. We got ahold of his phone, but there wasn't a video. So we looked on his laptop and sure enough, it was saved in his files. It was taken last September, according to the computer file, by the way." He says this last bit like it's insignificant information, even though we all know it's anything but. I'd already decided to trust Jace, but *man* does it feel good to have confirmation.

"Maybe he had the video but didn't send it?" I wonder. Yeah, I guess Annie was right. I'm a thinker.

"Did you ever get ahold of the girl whose phone it was sent from?" Jace asks.

"Wait, you found out whose cell phone it was?" I ask.

"Yeah, we had a buddy trace it," Wes tells me. "We'd never heard of the girl who owned the phone."

"Okay, James Bond, continue," I say, gesturing with my hand. "Did the girl know Wolfe?"

"At first she said no. But when we told her when the video was sent, she said some guy hit on her at a bar that night, asked for her phone number to call her later, and took an obscenely long time entering his own number into her phone. He said his name was Will, but when she looked for his number in her phone later, it wasn't there."

"And 'Will' had a shaved head and forehead scar just like Wolfe, I take it?" Jace asks.

"Yup."

"So now we need to handle Wolfe," Jace says darkly.

"Already handled," Wes tells him. He points to the grilled cheese on the skillet. "Is that ready?"

Jace picks it up and hands it to him on a spatula.

"What do you mean you already handled it?" Jace sounds irritated.

"Relax, man. The main priority isn't retaliation, but getting the fucker out of our lives, right?" Wes asks, hands up in surrender.

"We could have both," Jace answers. His jaw is clenched tight and I know he's already thinking of his next move.

"Hold it. The guy's crazy. I don't want to fuck with him and have him haunting me. Better to have something on him so he'll stay away. Recording that shit without your consent is a felony. Plus there's all kinds of civil shit you could go after him for."

Jace mulls this over. "I'd disagree that he shouldn't get away without retaliation. But he knows about Pepper now. And I don't want to risk him coming after her."

"Does Mad-Evil know it was Wolfe?" I ask.

Wes throws his head back in laughter. "You mean Brescoll? No, she doesn't know. Let's keep it that way."

"Yeah, she's as crazy as Wolfe. Who knows what she'd do? I just want this whole thing to be over with."

Jace puts his hands on my waist and pulls my legs around his hips. "It will be, Pep. No more fucking drama, okay?"

I smile and repeat his words. "No more fucking drama."

He laughs and leans in to speak softly in my ear, "I never thought you'd have to go through all this because you're my girlfriend, Pep. But you've handled it like a badass and I'm so proud of you."

His hot breath on my skin and the sincerity of his words make me squirm closer to him, wishing we were alone.

"Guys? Can you keep your hands off each other for two minutes?" Wes asks in mock anger. There's no mistaking the happiness on his face, though, when we turn to face him. I wonder if my friendship with Wes would have ended again if Jace and I broke up.

"Man, Pep, it's a good thing you didn't drag that out any longer. Jace was driving me nuts.

He's like a girl with his emotions when it comes to you." Wes shoves the rest of his grilled cheese into his mouth while keeping an eye on Jace in anticipation of another smack on the back of his head. But Jace doesn't seem inclined to pull away from me.

"Did you just dis girls?" I ask him in a threatening tone.

"Noooo... You're just taking it that way," Wes talks through a mouthful of food.

"Girls destroy furniture when they get upset?" Jace asks.

"Not this girl," I point to myself. "I run."

"That you do," Wes says. I think we're all reflecting on the snowstorm incident.

"You know," Jace comments. "I tried the running thing last week. Definitely didn't make me feel better."

"What about when you found me on the trail? That didn't help cheer you up?"

"A little better, but that was you, not the running. And I could tell you were still all bummed out and hurt so that didn't make me feel great."

"Yeah," I say on a sigh.

"Yeah," he repeats.

But that's all behind us now.

Chapter 22

After standing up to Madeline, it feels like nothing can come between Jace and me. Until that point, I was happy enough that we'd taken our friendship to the next level, but I think I struggled with how long it would last. I guess it was the "it's too good to be true" thing. There was always a little nagging doubt in my head, wondering if Jace would get tired of being in a relationship with me, or frustrated with monogamy. After all, despite his physical experience, I'm still his first girlfriend.

My doubts are gone now. And the more I reflect on it, the more I realize it wasn't so much Jace's past that fueled my lack of faith in us, but my own insecurities.

On the track before the last race of the two-day State meet, I shake out my arms and legs. It's a new thing I just started doing before races. It makes me feel like I'm shaking off the bad energy, any lingering insecurities. Yeah, I guess I have those on the track, too.

The leg and arm shake seemed to do the trick before the 4 x 800 last night. It was my first time running on the UC track. The college opened their facilities for the high school State Championship.

We placed third in the 4 x 800 – much better than we'd hoped. First place in the DMR is an ambitious goal, but we're fired up after the win at Districts two weeks ago, and for my part, I'm willing to lay it all out there.

Jenny and Zoe have switched relay legs. Jenny will be leading us out in the 1200, and Zoe's racing the 800. Jenny's faster in both events, and we can use that more to our advantage if she runs a longer leg. It will probably only gain us a second or two, but that's usually what it comes down to.

Jenny killed it in the finals for the mile earlier today, placing fifth amongst a highly competitive field. Her awesome race seems to have psyched her up for the relay, and she bounces on her feet before toeing the starting line with the rest of the first-leg relay runners.

Jenny surges forward and leads the pack for the first two laps before fatigue catches up to her. Runners start to pass her and she loses the lead. I was worried this would happen. She's starting to feel the effects from racing in the mile preliminaries and 4 x 800 yesterday, and then the mile finals again this morning. Despite how small she is, Jenny is one tough cookie. I can see her falter, getting ready to give in to the exhaustion, but she hangs on to the back of the lead pack as they round the last straightaway. She doesn't let anyone else pass her and I admire her determination.

Zippy takes off with the baton with four other runners just barely ahead. The top five relays have put a solid distance between the rest of the field. Zippy also had a packed two days of racing, but she's a senior with a lot of experience. She's done the multiple-day racing challenge before and proven she's got stamina.

One of the runners can't keep up with the quick pace and by the time the 400 leg comes around the curve to pass off the baton, there are only 4 teams in the lead pack.

Zoe raced the 2-mile yesterday but she's been laying low with me all day, waiting in anticipation for the DMR. She's got a decent 800, but she might have trouble maintaining our position in the lead pack. I'm not familiar with all the runners on the other teams, and some of them might be exhausted from earlier races, while others still have fresh legs, like me.

Zoe hangs in there on the first lap of the 2-lap leg but she begins to fade on the second lap. The team that fell behind on the last leg catches Zoe, and there's now a small gap between the two of them and the three teams who have pulled ahead. Nothing I can't handle.

I shake out my arms and legs one last time before positioning myself on the track to grab the baton from Zoe.

But as I jog forward and reach back for the handoff, the baton fumbles in my grasp and slips out of my hand. I stop mid-stride to retrieve it, nearly tripping over another runner taking her position for the handoff.

When it's firmly in my grasp, I take off and look ahead to examine the damage. I've lost a few seconds, but I'm not going to let the mistake ruin my race. It won't allow me to back down from reaching for first place. I make this clear to the crowd as I zoom forward, setting a pace that's more appropriate for an 800 race than the mile. But I've recently discovered the joy of testing my limits.

One lap into the race, and I'm passing the third place runner. She's fallen off from the other two. It's the same Everfield girl from Districts leading the field. Katerina Davis won the individual mile at Districts but placed second in it earlier today to the girl wearing red who is currently on her heels. The announcer is in his element as he highlights the rivalry between them that goes back to their freshman year.

When I surge past the leaders at the halfway point, the crowd realizes that this is no longer a race between the two rivals. Out of the corner of my eye I see people in the stands rise to their feet.

"Jones has taken the lead for Brockton Public. Davis and Cruz are trying to stay on her tail, but she's setting a brutal pace. If she can keep it up, we'll be seeing a new State record in the girls' DMR tonight."

Instead of crippling me, the mention of breaking a record lights a fire, and I push the pace even harder. Katerina Davis stays on me for half a lap before giving up. I'm in my element, letting the loud cheers fuel me.

I glance up to the foothills as I rip through the line into my last lap. The sun is setting on the horizon and the sky glows. I'm racing faster than I ever have, yet my legs glide along smoothly, showing no sign of letting up. If I wasn't using my mouth to suck in air, I'd be grinning.

When I float through the finish line, I'm told that Brockton Public holds the new State record in the DMR. It wouldn't have happened without my teammates, but for the first time, I feel like maybe I've earned the Brockton Public Phenomenon label. I'm not just an imposter.

I've proven that I have the courage to race like I own the track.

My smile widens when I look over the fence on the other side of the track and see Jace and Gran waving at me. Wes leans over the rail next to them, with Jim and Annie on his other side. That's my family over there. I might feel like I'm missing out on a traditional family, but it's the people watching me proudly on the other side of that fence who have proven they care about me. Even Annie, who came around a little late in the game, beams with pride.

With Zoe's arm around my shoulder, and my teammates surrounding me, I can't imagine feeling like I need anyone or anything else. It doesn't matter who tries to hurt me, I know exactly who I am and I will fight to protect what I have.

Made in the USA
Lexington, KY
11 August 2014